Masada Will Not Fall Again

University of Nebraska Press
Lincoln

MASADA
WILL NOT FALL AGAIN

A Novel

Sophie Greenspan

Illustrated by Unada

The Jewish Publication Society
Philadelphia

© 1973 by The Jewish Publication Society
of America

All rights reserved. Published by the University
of Nebraska Press as a Jewish Publication
Society book.

Library of Congress Control Number: 2018960162

For Sam

Contents

Masada Will Not Fall Again

To the Reader:

To help you in your understanding of this story
we have included a word list,
which you can find
at the end of the book.

Prologue

In the days when Rome was forging her empire on the shores of the Mediterranean, in the little kingdom of Judea, two brothers who were rivals for its throne appealed to the Roman emperor to settle their dispute. In the end, Judea was swallowed up into the Roman Empire.

But Judea proved to be an indigestible morsel for Rome. Rebellion flamed up all over the country, draining Rome of thousands of her soldiers and of vast sums of gold. In the long run, Roman strength proved too much for the Jews; both Jerusalem and the Galilee fell. Survivors of these rebellions made their way through the wastes of the Judean Desert for yet another stand at Masada, a natural fortress on the summit of a great rock overlooking the Dead Sea.

This fortress had been strengthened by a succession of rulers: first by Alexander Jannaeus (one of the line of Maccabean kings), then by Herod, and last by the Romans. A little time before our story, it had been won back by a famous guerrilla fighter called Menachem, who was a Zealot, one of those who had vowed to fight the Romans to the death. Now Masada was held by Menachem's nephew, Eleazar ben Ya'ir, a veteran of the Jewish revolt against the Romans.

Inspired by Israel's destiny, Jews in Israel and

outside its borders flocked to his side. We can imagine that there must have been people like our young married couple, Adin and Ohada from Babylonia; old Huldah and the young children: Iddo of the family of Temple priests, Aviel, and little Yitzhak, all from Jerusalem; the worldly Justus and his faithful convert wife, Sarah, from Alexandria, Egypt; the much-traveled Urzillah from Nabatea in the Negev; and Yeshu, the gentle Essene from Qumran.

Though diverse in their backgrounds and upbringing, in one essential they were alike. They were Zealots—and this is what united them under the intrepid leadership of Eleazar ben Ya'ir.

Then, as now, men dared to fight for freedom against terrible odds.

1 / Masada

The three travelers moved slowly toward it.

"Masada!"

The mountain lay before them like a giant ship whose keen prow had sliced into the red-yellow earth of the Judean Hills. Its head reared thirteen hundred feet above the hollows and peaks of the surrounding wasteland.

The Lord in His infinite wisdom had created Masada at this very point, but it was one man above all others who had shaped it further to suit his purposes. King Herod had loved the Greek way of life, and here the Greek imprint was plainly visible. To adorn the land of Israel with Greek art and architecture had become a passion to which he had devoted his whole life.

Why? So he could achieve the twofold aim of enjoying the luxuries of that civilization and at the same time flaunt to the world his success and power. Thirty-eight towers made of dolomite stone quarried on the spot, and hundreds of fluted columns with capitals in the form of Greek scrolls crowned the fortress of Masada, silhouetted against the intensely blue Judean skies above.

Ohada's eyes followed the lines of the structure from the top down to the rounded walls on the second level, one hundred feet below, then to its lowest level, which struck her as exquisitely beautiful.

Herod! The name always created argument whenever men gathered in council or even for friendly conversation. Was he a traitor or patriot? Now, standing at the base of the cliff, Ohada could only admire the skill and imagination of the man, villain though he might have been, who had dreamed of such a magnificent building. Castle and fortress— this was the palace of Masada, built with strength yet with grace and beauty, too.

"Too-oo-ooooooo!"

From the walls above, the call of the shofar warned of the approach of the little party. The guards on the walls had watched their coming and were now surrounded by a large group of people peering into the ravine.

The shofar! The thin, thrilling summons sounded

in Ohada's ears like the call of history. To her it was the trumpet blast of the Lord of Hosts who had stood on Mount Sinai to deliver the sacred Law. From Joshua to the Maccabees, the keening wail ran like a thread through the story of her people. Now once again the shofar would rally the Jews, this time in their battle against the mightiest foe of all times—the Romans.

Truly, thought Ohada, the Jewish people are among the most courageous. Theirs was the same blood as that of King David, and now it flowed in the veins of men like Eleazar ben Ya'ir, the commander of the fort above on the mountain. Ohada wondered if he was one of the people now looking down on them. Even in far-off Babylon, his deeds of bravery had reached their ears. What was he like, she wondered. Did he carry a sharp knife in his belt, like those who had earned for themselves the dread name of Sicarii: the daggered ones?

The three travelers in the Nahal Sebbeh sank down on the sun-warmed rocks and waited for permission to proceed. It would be dangerous to go farther. Already bows were being bent on the battlements above. Who was to know whether these newcomers were friend or foe? Rome had her spies.

Ohada sat near Adin. As always, a feeling of strength and reassurance seemed to flow from him. Only through his constant determination had she been able to complete the long journey begun in Nahardea of Babylon so many months ago and now ending with the tiresome and monotonous stretch from Qumran on the west bank of the Asphalt Sea, as some called the Dead Sea.

Yeshu sat alone on a rock at a little distance from the couple, as though still showing his preference for the lonely life he had led with the Essenes in the stark desert outpost of Qumran. His delicate hand rested on the jars containing the scrolls he had brought with him. They were a small remnant of his community's library, which he and others of his sect had hidden in caves upon the approach of the Romans. One of the scrolls was Ecclesiasticus, written by the sage Ben-Sira. From this master, Yeshu had learned that true wisdom is the revelation of God. From the words of this teacher, Yeshu had guided and shaped his life— a life devoted to piety of mind and discipline of body.

In his other hand, Yeshu carried the Book of Jubilees. To Ohada it made difficult reading because it was written in Hebrew, while her mother tongue was Aramaic. However, she could understand and love the stories when Yeshu read them aloud to her. Written down by the Qumran sect, they were the legends that told about the adventures of Father Abraham in his wanderings through the land of Mesopotamia into the land of Canaan—the very journey she had, in fact, just completed herself. How these stories had enlivened the evenings in the ruins of Qumran and helped her over the thirty long miles to Masada!

Adin stirred by her side. Ohada looked up at his face. Little was said between them. The impressive rock that lay before them, the loneliness of the place, and their tiredness kept them silent. Indeed, there was not much need for words. Their marriage had stood up against the opposition of their families, who had forbidden the trip and had foretold the dangers that lay before them. The separation from their families had been difficult, and the young people missed the relatives who had begged them to remain with them in the security of Babylonia.

Now the touch of her hand on Adin's seemed to say, "Our journey is over!"

His answering smile spoke more than words.

He offered her a drink from the goatskin container he carried over his shoulder: spring water from the wells of Ein Gedi. Ohada refused, as did Yeshu. The sight of their goal drove all thought of thirst or discomfort from their minds.

Two figures could be distinguished coming down the white path that led from the summit to what seemed to be the midpoint between the northern and southern ends of the rock. The travelers began to move toward the men coming to meet them.

Surely neither goats nor gazelles could have managed the descent more gracefully than these Zealots. On their backs, bow and quiver swung to the rhythm of their movement. Sliding frequently, they propelled themselves rapidly and skillfully down the pebbly tracks. Tied around their waists were plaited ropes, which they had brought to aid those less experienced than themselves. On their feet were heavy Roman-style sandals, with broad straps that protected and strengthened the ankles.

At the base of the path, the mountaineers reached for their bows and arrows before advancing boldly toward the three travelers.

"Who are you and what do you seek?"

The question was addressed to all, but it was Ohada, always impulsive, who answered first.

"I am Ohada, the daughter of Ezra, a scribe of Nahardea. I have come here to take part in the struggle for the freedom of my people Israel from the yoke of the Romans."

She spoke quickly and firmly. The words came without hesitation because she had long formulated them in her mind. All during the wearisome journey she had repeated to herself the purpose of her venture. Thus had she borne the rigors and perils, growing more steadfast in her convictions.

The interrogator's eyes turned to Adin. Adin spoke simply in few words.

"I have come to fight for my people. This was part of the vows of marriage that Ohada, daughter of Ezra, and I made to each other on our wedding day."

Ohada flashed her husband a grateful smile.

Now it was Yeshu's turn, and the words burst forth like a spring suddenly freed.

"My name is Yeshu of the Qumran sect. At the time the Kittim, cursed be their name, captured Qumran, I was absent taking a message from the brethren to Ein Gedi. I returned to find the settlement in ruins. I have come to avenge the blood of my brethren, and I will take up the sword with the Sicarii of Masada. It is written in our book, *The Manual of Discipline,* that the Sons of Darkness will be annihilated. I believe that there will be a victory of the just over the wicked."

The vision of Yeshu bearing a sword caused a half-smile to appear on the lips of one of the youths, but it disappeared quickly as he said, "Blessed are you who come in the name of the Lord."

And then, hungry for the news of the outside world, the two young warriors let the questions come tumbling forth. They spoke Aramaic, the language common to all Jews of the time.

"What news of the Galilee?"

"What news of our brethren who are scattered in the lands of the Romans? Will they come to help us, or will they listen to the lies of the traitor Josephus?"

"Will they come to fight the heathen or remain in their comfortable homes in the empire of the eagle?"

Adin responded explosively.

"The Galilee! The Lord has forsaken us in the Galilee. The dark days before the coming of the Messiah have come. Now there is only Masada. Here in Masada, we, with the help of God, will prove that the people of the Book have not been forsaken. Masada will be the instrument of God. Here for the greater glory of God we will make our stand and drive out the accursed Romans. We will chastise them like dogs."

Ohada was filled with pride to hear her husband speak out so courageously. The child in her womb stirred for the first time at that moment. To Ohada it came as an omen. God had given her a sign of hope. It would be a boy, she determined, and the boy would live to see Israel a free nation. She would name him Yehudah, after the Maccabee who had freed the Jewish people from the idol-worshiping Greeks.

A recollection of her grandmother came to her mind. How she had lived with memories of her people and how she would have cherished this moment! The family of Ohada had returned to the land that had been the beginning and the fulfillment of the Jewish people.

Ohada silently blessed this moment.

"Blessed art Thou, O Lord, King of the universe, who hast kept us alive and sustained us and brought us to this moment!"

2 / Between Heaven and Earth

For Ohada, the first days of Masada were like a dream. If, as many believed, the heaven that lay above them was the abode of God, then surely Massada was close to heaven and she was close to God. The blue sky was so bright and pure and clean that it seemed she had only to stretch out her hand to touch it. Here one could truly believe with the Pharisees that there would be an afterlife for the righteous, as a reward for their devotion to God while they were on earth. How cold the Sadducees seemed with their insistence that nothing followed this earthly existence!

The atmosphere in the community was tense; war stood on their very doorstep. Perhaps because of that, Ohada found a special consolation and beauty in the prayers during her first Sabbath on Masada.

The day began with the service in the synagogue whose roof was the sky. The synagogue lay directly to the left of what had been Herod's private palace. Sitting on the edge of the amphitheater, Ohada enjoyed an eagle's view of austere beauty. The prayers were oriented toward Jerusalem, on which the thoughts of the congregation dwelt constantly. By turning her head to the east, Ohada could see the red of the mountains of Moab. In between, the rays of the sun played on the dull, salt waters of the Dead Sea far below. It resembled a mirror of polished metal, and she fancied that it had been clouded over by the breath of the divine Creator.

Her eyes followed the cleft of the Jordan Valley; many miles to the northwest lay the city for which she yearned, now captive under the heel of the alien Kittim. Never had she been privileged to see the city of Mount Zion, the work of Yedidiah, whose other name was Solomon, lover of God. His buildings had been erased and now lay in shambles on the holy mount. Never would she be able to wend her way three times a year, as pilgrims had done for countless centuries, to the very center of the world—Jerusalem.

Eleazar ben Ya'ir stood in the men's section, his talit over his head as his deep voice affirmed the hope that Jerusalem would be rebuilt speedily. His words seemed to form a vow to regain the Holy City. Thus at the same time would he avenge the death of his uncle, Menachem. Was Eleazar covering his eyes to drive out the awful sight of his uncle naked and writhing silently under the lashes of the *flagrum,* the whip with chains, that a grinning Roman was bringing down on the pulp that was once a proud, living man? Was Eleazar seeing again the faces of the Romans standing in square formation and enjoying the sight of a man being humiliated and tortured? Was Eleazar deliberately trying to imprint on his memory the scene of his uncle's flayed and mangled body stretched on the crude cross for all to see?

Jerusalem! How had the mighty fallen! It was a haunting nightmare. Ohada's mind shied away from the frightful picture the remembrance brought up in the mind of every Jew. Beside her on the women's benches sat women and children still bearing the signs of the suffering and starvation they had endured during the long siege. Rats and mice were the food of the poor people, and desperate mothers had searched the refuse heaps for any scraps that might serve to still for a while the crying of their hungry children.

Rounded, bloated bellies and thin sticklike legs were not easily mended. It was a wonder—indeed, a miracle—that such little legs had been able to make the trek across the Judean Hills, a difficult journey for both man and beast. Some miracle of God had carried these children through to Masada.

Ohada breathed a silent prayer that the baby she was carrying would bring redemption to Israel and a new world of peace for all mankind. Surely the Creator would make the cause of light prevail over the powers of darkness and evil. Some men gave this evil power the name of Satan. Yeshu believed with the Essenes that the spirit of impurity was the spirit of Satan. In fact, like all Essenes, he prayed every day: "Let Satan and an impure spirit not rule over me and let not pain or evil inclinations claim power over my bones."

White-shawled Pharisees and Essenes draped in their robes of white, together with hard-bitten Zealots, rose together to honor the return of the scrolls of the Law to the ark. Then the congregation slowly filed out into the open area of the camp. As they strolled down the short path that led to the northern wall, Ohada and Adin caught a glimpse of the Western

Path over which they had made their ascent on that fateful night. Every detail of the climb remained etched in their memory.

At the suggestion of the guards and to make it easier for Ohada, they had waited for the fierce sun of the month of Elul to set before beginning the steep climb. By the time they had completed the ascent, the mystery of the night lay before them and around them, and the harvest moon had reached its full power. Baruch and Nachum, the guards, had relieved them of their burdens, leaving the newcomers free to grasp the rocks whenever the footing was unsure. With Baruch leading the way and Nachum bringing up the rear, the two guards were always on hand when help was needed. They toiled to the top. The chorus of jackals yapping from the surrounding desert reminded the climbers that danger threatened those who allowed themselves to become weak. But the desert lizards that scurried between their feet gave them the comforting feeling that nature was playing friendly pranks on them.

At the point where the path suddenly rose at an increased angle, Baruch insisted that the ropes be used to insure safety. They went up hand over hand, until finally the watchman at the top, who had kept himself informed at all times of the progress of the climbers, came out to assist the little party over the last stretch.

Eager hands helped Ohada over the walls, and she was bundled off to the campfire burning in the center of the compound between the encircling buildings. Quickly the others joined her. Ohada was awed by the tall, fluted Greek columns topped by the scrolls, which she now saw close at hand.

Bowls of hot broth appeared like magic in their hands, and Ohada sipped the liquid gratefully, her eyes feasting meanwhile on the beautiful surroundings, which were in keeping with the Greek pattern that she had first seen when she stood in the wadi below just ten hours before.

A natural simplicity and inherent politeness showed in the behavior of the defenders. There was warmth but no weak sentimentality in the manner in which they were received. Everyone was calm and matter-of-fact. Scarcely a word had been spoken as the newcomers had climbed over the parapet, but the sentry on duty and others afterward searched their faces carefully as though seeking someone from former times.

Were they hoping to find members of their family lost in the disaster that had killed thousands of Jews in the Galilee and in Jerusalem, that had separated families and friends? There were no signs of recognition, but their hosts on Masada did not show their disappointment and turned to the newcomers with tenderness and kindness.

When they had finished eating, the three were taken to one of the buildings where cots had been set up for them. Weary, yet strangely excited and exhilarated, the travelers threw themselves onto their beds of leather stretched over wooden frames. They covered themselves with blankets made of sheep's wool and fell asleep immediately.

Peaceful days followed in dreamy succession, yet Ohada and Adin knew that this was only the peace before the storm. Scouts from the northern Galilee brought reports that the Romans were preparing an immense army, which would be sent out to attack the

Zealots. But this attack would not come for a while. In the meantime, there was in the fortress an air of certainty and confidence. All worked hard during the weekdays, strengthening their position. But on the Sabbath, toil ceased and the community rested.

Couples strolled along the perimeter enjoying the magnificent view. Ohada and Adin chose a rock overlooking the Dead Sea. From there they gazed in fascination at the beautiful panorama of the inland sea. Suddenly their contemplation was interrupted by somebody calling.

"Ohada! Adin!"

The voice came from the wall. They turned and saw a young woman. She drew near them.

"I have been told that you are from Nahardea. I seek news of the family of Yoram, son of Avram, who was my father's brother. Perhaps you knew him in Nahardea. He was a teacher and also worked in metals."

Adin and Ohada looked at each other in pleased surprise. This was a link with home. The memories of their youth in Babylonia were happy ones, and they liked to tell about them.

"Come," said Ohada, seating the young woman between them. "I think you speak of the scribe who taught my husband and my brothers in the schools of our city."

"We loved him dearly," Adin said, "and we learned much in his school. He was one who gave us a love for the Holy Land, and it was he who helped us decide to come here."

As they replied to the young woman's eager questions, their old home and this new one began to merge in their minds. The Jewish homes and schools of Babylon had kept the links of Jewish continuity strong and unbroken.

3/Yeshu and Aviel

There was an old proverb the boy Aviel had often heard his elders use. Afterward he realized that he should have been guided by its wisdom when he had first met Yeshu: "Don't judge the wine by the jug it's in."

It had been impossible to judge Yeshu's real worth from his outward appearance. When Yeshu entered the fort in the company of Adin and Ohada he had not been understood. His thin, pinched features seemed always to be covered with an expression of gloom. Conditions in the camp were serious enough without making them seem worse, and people were repelled by his sour appearance. His body was spindly and awkward, and he did not look like a warrior; nor did it seem possible that he could make any sort of contribution to the battle ahead. The tough fighting men of the fort did not doubt his sincerity in coming to fight with them, but they regarded him with amusement.

Yeshu did not help them to understand his real character. Had he allowed them to come closer to him and had he encouraged friendship, they would have found that under the thin, pinched exterior there was a man of unusual warmth and love of humanity. They would have discovered, too, that he had been trained as a fighter and knew the rules of combat as laid out in *The Manual of Discipline* of the Essenes. But Yeshu kept everyone at arm's length, discouraging companionship and preferring to remain silent whenever he found himself in the company of people.

Even while eating with the community at the religious ceremonies, he seemed removed from it all. He sat by himself, slowly chewing small mouthfuls of the portion that lay before him. He never spoke to anyone while eating and never touched meat or fish. He seemed to be content with small helpings, and he picked his diet from the fruits and vegetables, which, together with the bread, satisfied his hunger. When the meal was over, he led the group in the Grace after Meals, which he chanted with great reverence.

He added the words, "A youth was I and now I am an old man, and I have never seen the righteous abandoned by the Lord." This was an Essene addition to the Grace that was unfamiliar to a great many of the people of Masada. But because it added a note of optimism for the future, it soon became an established part of the Grace for everyone.

The boys of the camp naturally modeled themselves after the warriors, particularly ben Ya'ir, and they tended to regard Yeshu as a figure to be mocked. One of these boys, Aviel, who lived with his family in a casemate room next to Yeshu, soon had something to report to his playmates. Spying through a crack in the wall between the apartments one morning, he saw something that amused him very much. Yeshu was immersing himself in a tub that stood in the center of the room. Only his thin hair floated above the water in the tub. Then he emerged from his ablutions, shivering in the cold morning air, and dressed himself in his white clothing.

Aviel thought the whole scene was really funny —the thin, shivering body, the spindly legs, and above all the serious expression on the face of the bather.

Aviel did not know that this was an important rite in the religious practices of the Essenes. By bathing they symbolically purified themselves from sin and then tried in every moment of their day to keep themselves righteous in all their actions. And Aviel did not realize until afterward how thoughtful Yeshu was in all his deeds. He had brought the bath water from the southern cistern by himself so that the women would not be put to extra work.

When Aviel ran out to share his discovery with his friends, the unsuspecting Yeshu began the next stage of his morning ritual: he put on his phylacteries and commenced the recital of the morning prayers. His ascetic features were still set in the same serious mood of contemplation.

Aviel had no patience with lengthy rituals. Eleazar was his idol, and he knew that Eleazar did not go in for so much prayer. Had he paid more attention, however, Aviel would have noticed that Eleazar showed great respect for Yeshu, whom he considered not only a good and righteous man but also a brave man who would fight for his convictions when the time came.

Aviel had a problem of his own that he did not care to share with anyone. It was something that could not be changed, something he would have to bear all his life. Though Iddo, another boy in the

colony, was not to blame, he was the one who brought the problem to a head each time.

Aviel had watched Iddo's entrance into the community. The newcomer was a survivor from Jerusalem, and had come into the camp sometime after Aviel. He had evidently suffered the same hardships that all Jerusalem had undergone, but somehow he had been able to withstand them better. Perhaps this was because he belonged to a wealthy section of the priesthood; perhaps he had been fortunate in having the proper food when he was very young. His frame was powerful, and it seemed that he had been able to draw on the reserves of strength built up in his early years. Even when he first stepped into the fort from the hard climb up the Snake Path, Iddo was already capable of sharing in the work of the camp without needing to recuperate from privation.

He was, indeed, the strongest boy in the colony. Not yet twelve, he could bend a bow like a man, roll heavy stones with the warriors, and carry heavy burdens. Iddo was the leader of the boys in all games of strength, especially in the game of rider-on-horseback. In this game one boy would mount another and try to bring down a similar pair in a hand-to-hand contest. The stronger the rider, the better their chances for winning. But the team also needed a very strong "horse," and Iddo was especially suited to being a horse. When he entered the game with his rider, no one could stand up against them. It was always the others who went down to defeat.

Aviel's ambition was to outdo Iddo, but Iddo seemed unconquerable. Besides, Aviel had a handicap he tried to conceal. One of his legs was weak. But he did not want anyone to notice it, so he did not talk about it at all.

After the fall of Jerusalem his family had managed to escape from the Romans and were making their way through the Judean Desert. Traveling in the month of Tamuz, when the sun is at its hottest, and weakened by starvation and a shortage of water, the little family struggled across the stony wastes. Aviel could still remember how his tongue swelled in his mouth from lack of water, and how a crust of dryness had formed around his mouth. In spite of his father's supporting arm, he staggered from weakness and wanted only to lie down to end it all. Then came that awful night. While he was lying on the bare ground one night, a scorpion had crawled up his leg; when he tried to brush it off, the creeping thing had stung him. His father came quickly when Aviel cried out in pain, and tried to suck out the poison from the wound; but in spite of that the leg swelled up.

The family was now in an even worse position than before because Aviel had to be carried all the rest of the way. Carrying the baby was enough of a burden; carrying Aviel would have been beyond the strength of his weakened parents.

The family was immobilized in the desert and on the verge of despair. They gave themselves up for dead. The wild creatures in the area, sensing their hopelessness, prowled around them all night. In the evening, a band of wandering Arabs of the Rechabite tribe found them. For centuries these Arabs had practiced the hospitality of Abraham, from whom they claimed descent. They took Aviel and his family into their tent encampment, where he stayed until his leg was somewhat healed. But from that day on, Aviel walked with a slight limp when he was tired.

It was something that disturbed him, and he wanted to forget it. But it was always brought to mind when he tried to match his strength against Iddo's. When Aviel finally realized after many tries that he would never win a test of physical skill with Iddo, he decided to resort to cunning.

One day the boys decided to play capture-the-fort. Aviel and Iddo were the captains of the opposing forces. Iddo's side would man the fort and Aviel's would have the task of taking it from them. To outwit the enemy, Aviel planned to make a sudden secret attack. First, however, his men must conceal themselves from Iddo's view and wait. While Iddo was searching through every part of the compound, Aviel and his men would hide outside the walls surrounding Masada until they could spring upon the "enemy" and take them by surprise. Aviel and his men had gotten the idea from the way Menachem had taken the fort of Masada from the Romans by stealth.

The strategy seemed to be going well. Peering cautiously over the wall, Aviel saw that Iddo and his gang had left their fort and were searching the casemate chambers and the other buildings of the camp. Aviel stationed his men behind the rocks while he hung on the wall, watching. Impatiently they waited for their opponents to go over to the north wall. That would give Aviel's team time to skip through the west gate and seize the fort. How Aviel would laugh when Iddo returned to find him sitting at the captured fort!

But time seemed endless. Their opponents searched every nook and cranny, and Aviel's fingers were getting numb. Then disaster struck at Aviel's weakest point. He had brought along little Yitzhak because Hannah, Yitzhak's grandmother, had insisted. Aviel had protested, knowing from past experience that the six-year-old was not capable of playing with the older boys.

So when Aviel heard a cry behind him, he was not surprised to find that it was Yitzhak who had called. He had slipped and rolled down the slope. Fortunately, he had been stopped by a large rock. Had he fallen farther he would have gone off into the canyon and been killed. But Aviel's relief did not last long. He saw that the child was struggling to get up and could not do so. Something had happened to his leg.

Aviel had learned in his short life how to face a crisis. He forgot Iddo and the game. Now there was nothing in his mind but fear—fear that little Yitzhak's leg would be like his own. With horror Aviel realized that he was the unwitting cause of Yitzhak's accident. He had brought him out on the cliff; the blame was his and his alone.

Aviel quickly told his second-in-command, a boy somewhat smaller than himself, to watch Yitzhak while he went for help. Luckily for them, however, they did not have to wait. Yeshu had heard the cries of little Yitzhak from the other side of the casemate wall and had come out by way of the west gate to see what had happened.

Never had anyone seemed so welcome to Aviel as this pinched, sour-looking Yeshu. As he bent over the injured boy, Yeshu's expression was one of love and tenderness. Carefully, he probed the leg and ankle and then took the little one up in his arms.

Yitzhak was still sobbing with pain as Yeshu laid him down on the bare cot in his room, sent the children outside, and began a closer examination. Aviel, watching from the doorway, was comforted when he saw Yeshu turn away from the child with an expression of calm assurance on his face. Then, taking a piece of linen, Yeshu dipped it into a jar where he kept his fresh water. From another jar, he produced some herbs and then proceeded to bind up the ankle with the damp rag. He repeated the process on the other ankle.

Aviel could wait no longer. He had to know if Yitzhak was all right or if the boy was to be crippled for life. Aviel broke down and sobbed out his words, big tears coursing down his cheeks.

"Yeshu, tell me that he will be all right. Tell me that I didn't harm Yitzhak. Tell me that his legs will be straight again. I will pray to God three times a day, and I will submerge myself in cold water every morning if it will only help Yitzhak."

Yeshu stood transfixed. He knew from these words that Aviel must have been watching him at his morning ablutions. But he soon recovered himself and said in a reassuring voice, "We have all to thank God. Yitzhak was spared by His divine mercy. We will apply herbs and put his leg in a very firm bandage. The rest will be in God's hands. In the course of time we hope that he will be able to use his two legs."

Aviel was trying to say how grateful he was to Yeshu and to God when he was interrupted by the stormy entrance of Hannah. Hannah was habitually a prey to anxiety; now she was beside herself. The young orphan—entrusted to her when his mother,

Hannah's daughter, died in Jerusalem—had been injured. How badly she did not know. She was ready to blame anybody and everybody.

She made sure that Yitzhak was alive, then turned her wrath on Aviel, whom she held responsible for the mishap.

Once again, Yeshu was able to save Aviel—this time from the tongue-lashing that broke over him. Hardly had she started, when he lifted Yitzhak and carried him to her room. The old lady was forced to stop her tirade against Aviel to follow close upon Yeshu's heels. She walked as quickly as her old legs would let her, alternately calling out endearing names to her grandson and screaming angrily backward at Aviel.

As the days went by, Aviel tried to show his gratitude to Yeshu, but it was hard to find the proper words. He was reminded that he had scoffed and even mimicked the old man's walk and his ways. What made it extra hard was that Yeshu had never reprimanded him. Now Yeshu seemed to Aviel like a saint who walked among men completely undeterred by sins or sinners and serenely untouched by them. Aviel's conscience was sorely troubled.

It was while visiting little Yitzhak later and playing a game to amuse him that he really came to know Yeshu. The boys had been playing shadow-on-the-wall. Aviel had formed a shadow of a wolf's head with his hands when a howl came from outside. It sounded exactly like the cry of a wolf.

Into the doorway stepped Yeshu. He had a smile on his face as his mouth continued to make the wolf call. His face broke into more smiles when he saw the surprised look on the faces of the boys. They had never associated Yeshu with tricks and games.

Yeshu had come to take the bandages off the ankles of the little patient. Aviel had the satisfaction of seeing Yitzhak's leg almost unmarred by the accident. He watched Yitzhak take a few slow steps while Yeshu held him.

Yeshu had some time free afterward so he stayed to talk. He answered the children's questions about the life at Qumran.

"Weren't you lonesome without your family?"

"What work did you do there?"

"Did you live there at the time the man Jesus was there?"

"Was there really a man called Jesus?"

"Did you really keep quiet all the time, without talking to your friends?"

Yeshu told them all about Qumran. After that, Aviel became a frequent visitor at Yeshu's apartment. He learned to love this gentle man.

Frequently Yeshu had time to read to them from the scrolls of Ben-Sira. Many an hour was spent in learning the proverbs of this great sage.

"The beginning of wisdom is knowing God."

"The beginning of pride is when one departeth from God."

"Everything is in the hands of God except the choice of good or evil."

"Let thy lips be sincere—be swift to hear the words of the wise and to learn from them."

"He who keepeth the Law bringeth offering enough."

The face of Aviel sometimes took on the serious

expression of Yeshu as he pondered questions of right and wrong. Ben-Sira made one think hard about one's behavior. Yeshu promised Aviel that he would teach him how to read well so that he could read from the books himself.

Aviel looked forward to the time when he could unroll the scrolls and read his favorite story about Abraham and his dream of the angels. In his mind, as Yeshu read the story, he saw Yeshu as Father Abraham. Aviel thought he was magnificent.

4 / "Pax Romana"

"Pax Romana!"

The words were spat from the mouth of a Zealot standing on the cliff area behind the great northern castle. Hate and scorn colored the words of the speaker, as he watched the approach of the Roman siege army below.

"If they send twenty-five thousand troops to bring peace, how many should we expect if they should decide to make war with us?"

Ohada recognized the speaker. He was Justus, one of the survivors of the massacre of the Jews in Alexandria in Egypt. These men had all witnessed atrocities perpetrated by the Romans. Their words revealed the bitter humor of men who were trying to keep sane in the face of hideous memories that remained with them in their waking hours and filled their sleep with nightmares.

"The cursed swine have not been wasting their time," said one of the Zealots. "Think of the preparation needed to put an army of this size in front of us."

"Paid for, no doubt, by the jewels and treasures of our families," said another.

The great noise of their coming was symbolic of the Roman determination to put an end to the Jewish rebellion. The stillness of the Judean wilderness echoed with the march of a military power that shook the ground. Dust rose in great waves from the vast movement below.

The Roman eagle floated on tall standards over the orderly array.

"Heaven help us!" It was the prayer of Ohada.

"Heaven will help us, but we will have to do our share to help heaven," came the answer of Justus. "For this have we waited and for this were we destined. The Lord has brought them here in their might so that we may destroy the forces of Satan all together."

His words drew an approving nod from Eleazar, the Jewish commander who was intently watching the Roman army.

Despite the hovering dust, the formation of the army below was clearly visible to the watchers on the mountain.

The order of the Roman army on the march followed a pattern that never changed. Everything was carefully set out according to plan. And at the end of the day's march of twenty miles, the camp the army erected was built exactly like the camp they had left behind. Whether the campaign took place in Britain, in Gaul, or in Palestine, the Roman army was governed by the same procedure.

The ensigns and banners identified the various units in the legion. Towering over all was the siege train with its towers.

"Our beautiful Lebanon cedars!"

"They lay waste our land to make engines of war!"

"How Solomon would have cried at the loss of his trees!"

The arrogant parade of Roman might continued. The infantry, consisting of ranks of six men marching shoulder to shoulder in tight formation, stretched in endless columns. They were dressed in brown leather from shoulder to knee, with scarlet kilts below their cuirasses. Each bore a cowhide shield that protected him from neck to knee. Its oblong frame was stretched over iron, and it was carried by a handle that slipped over the soldier's left hand. His right hand lay ready for the sword at his side.

On the back of each soldier was a full marching pack weighing sixty pounds. These heavy packs contained the basket, the pickax, and the saw and hatchet needed for digging. In addition there were sufficient provisions for three days' march and three pickets for the fortification that would have to be built at their next camp site.

They moved with precision at a regular pace, their sturdy legs protected with leather greaves and their feet in stout-thonged sandals. The total image was that of a large brown creature moving relentlessly toward its prey on many legs. But the headpieces of iron, brightly burnished and shining in the afternoon sun, showed clearly that these were indeed Roman troops on the march.

Protecting these foot soldiers were columns of cavalrymen mounted on magnificent Spanish horses, their tasseled helmets swaying with the motion of the horses they rode.

Would the line never stop? The Tenth Legion had a personal grudge against the cursed Jews in front of them. The memory of the shame the legion had suffered at the hands of the Jews in the siege of Jerusalem still rankled in the minds of the troops. To the

watchers on the hill, the Tenth Legion brought back the memory of the flogging and the crucifixion of Menachem and of thousands of others—scenes of horror that could never be forgotten.

Shame covered the faces of the Jews on the hill as they watched the next contingent. Thousands of laborers moved by, as well as servants carrying the luggage of the officers. These servants attended to the comfort of the officers wherever the legion was encamped. Among all these were Jews who had chosen a life of servitude rather than death on the cross. A live dog is better than a dead lion, they had reasoned. So they wore the brown sackcloth of a slave and toiled for their masters.

Now came the officers on their huge horses. Contempt showed in their faces for the people who dared to defy them. The officers wore gilded armor and red-plumed helmets. Their leader, Silva, had been promoted to the position of procurator of Judea. He was a hardened veteran of the siege of Jerusalem, where he had served with Titus.

He had a task to perform, and he was determined to accomplish it quickly. For how could you convince the Romans at home that Pax Romana prevailed in Palestine when news was constantly trickling out regarding the persistent guerrilla activities of the Jews? There would be many red faces among the government officials in Rome who had struck the coins with the words *"Judaea capta"*—Judea taken—if they knew that the Judeans were still a force to be reckoned with!

The pride of the Roman Empire rested on the outcome of this campaign against the stubborn Jews of Masada. Silva did not underestimate the caliber of the men who now faced him on the mountain fortress. They were, he knew, a hardened band determined to use this resistance as the beginning of a new period of rebellion. This battle, they hoped, would cause the people to arise in another mighty war that would sweep the Romans out of their land.

The dust of the march became denser as the columns were replaced by the large machines of war. Of these, the great siege towers were most prominent. Close behind them were the cranes, which would be used to lift great burdens. Slung between mules were powerful rams. Their purpose in the siege would be to batter and pound the walls of the fort. Trundling along on little wheels behind these rams were the catapults, which would hurl mighty stones into the besieged fort.

Everywhere along the columns, scouts on horses galloped their mounts like fussy nurses guarding their wards from the dangers that lay along the way.

Water-carriers, clad in sand-colored sacking, bent under the skin bags they carried on their backs as they marched. The cooks plodded along in the dust. Over these, too, the line of scouts hovered like soldier ants covering the line of march of worker ants on the move. A mule train carried sacks of grain and skins of wine. Plenty of porridge and coarse barley bread gave the soldiers their energy.

At the end a rear guard of light infantry marched along, followed by a detachment of heavy infantry. Four units of swift rear-guard cavalry insured the safety of all.

The march was ended; the goal of the hard journey had been reached. The line of march had now passed the full length of the fortress, and the scouts gave the signal to halt.

All motion ceased. Here the road ended.

Just three months before, this road had been a trail. Ohada had traveled along that trail. Now it was paved—a road built on a bed of crushed stone and cement, by Roman engineers. Its curbs insured good drainage in case of rain. It led straight to the horizon, undaunted by hill or valley. This was the Roman road —the symbol of Roman efficiency. It had brought the army to Masada and would serve to bring additional troops and supplies as the need arose. Along this road, messages would go forth to Rome, reporting on the progress of the army. Roman communications had triumphed again. It was true that "all roads lead to Rome."

Silva ascended a stage that his engineers had prepared and spoke to his troops.

"Soldiers of the great city of Rome: Before us lies Masada. In it lurk a handful of miserable barbarians, taking shelter in a last stand. I call them 'barbarians' as does their own historian Josephus Flavius. For they refuse to accept the comfort and protection of our great emperor. They refuse to learn the lesson of Carthage. Carthage—the great city—refused to accept the blessings of Rome. Now Masada tries to defy our army. Like the frog in the fable, these Jews blow themselves up, trying to become as large as an ox. Masada tries to do what Carthage could not do. Let Masada beware.

"Gallant soldiers, your standards above you bear the letters SPQR, setting you apart as the men espe-

cially chosen by the Senate and the people of Rome as the representatives of a great power—the greatest power of this time and of all times before this. As the letters indicate, you have been honored by Rome to bring its message to the world. And what is this message? It is simply stated: the people of Rome want to live in peace with the people of all other countries and to trade and do business with them.

"And since these obstinate wretches before us refuse to accept Roman kindness, we are forced to bring them the sword. Since they do not choose the Roman way of life, offered to them in all good faith, we must come to them with the power of Roman might. Perhaps they will still realize the great benefits that Rome can give them. If not, they will have to share the fate of Carthage and Jerusalem."

A great shout rose from the throats of the twenty-five thousand men before Silva.

Though Eleazar could not hear the words of the speech, he could imagine what was being said to the soldiers below. He turned his strong, thoughtful features from the Romans and spoke firmly to his band of Zealots. They followed every word with great attention. Eleazar knew his men and their ideals.

"Heroes of Masada, proud descendants of the tribe of Levi, and of the Hasmoneans, Hyrcanus, and Jonathan! We have been chosen as the instrument of God. It has been told us how in the end of days, the forces of light will meet with the forces of darkness in a final battle before the coming of the Messiah. The words of our prophets are now being revealed to us. Will we be worthy of our people and of our God? This mighty parade has been put on to place fear in our hearts. But whom should we fear? Should we be afraid of idolaters? When Solomon, beloved of God, built the House of the Lord on Mount Zion, these pigs were groveling in caves and eating raw meat like savages. Our forefathers knew how to fight long before Silva became a conqueror. We had our Joshua, who led the people of Israel against the mighty Jebusites, taking the land even unto Hazor in the north. Whom should we fear? These people who nurtured a Herod—he who shed the blood of forty-five innocent members of his own family?

"Here in Masada we will not give our young men to the idolaters, will not fill their amphitheaters with fighters to amuse them, while people like Josephus sit in the galleries and watch Roman 'culture.' Jewish blood will not flow for their amusement. Our faith is strong, It is God we worship. We will not accept the eagle or the ways of the eagle.

"Our choice is clear. The eagle—or the Lord who created all things. Which will it be?"

Eleazar spoke from his heart. His keen blue eyes sought out the faces of his band to see whether his words expressed their thoughts. He saw and felt the warmth and adoration of the young people Adin and Ohada, standing not far from Baruch and Nachum, who had brought them over the Western Path on their entrance into Masada. He had no difficulty in picking out the strong-featured Justus, whose determination matched his features. But Eleazar's glance lingered longer on the face of the Essene Yeshu. In his expression he read the resolve of a man dedicated to a divine mission on this mountain fastness.

Eleazar continued.

"We will yet bring to the Temple our offerings—the offerings that we have never ceased collecting. Our tithes will go there with the holy articles we were able to salvage from the destruction, which you have brought here from Jerusalem. The day of redemption will come in our time."

The shouts that rose from the battlements were a direct response to the challenge thrown down by Silva. Yeshu's voice rose above the others. "God's will be done!"

5 / Urzillah, Child of the Negev

Everything about Urzillah seemed so different, yet so right. She was the spirit of adventure. Her life, her background, her appearance, and her way of speaking and acting—all these were a delight to everyone.

The very way she had come into the camp—the last of the stragglers to join her people at Masada—sounded as romantic as the story of Jonah and the whale or Daniel in the fiery furnace. She had slipped in while the defenders were watching the Romans encamp on the west side of the fort. She had made her way up the Snake Path on the side facing the Dead Sea when everyone's attention was turned to the west. The fact that she had climbed the cliff alone was not half as astonishing as the story she told about her journey through Nabatea.

Urzillah was a Jewish maiden whose people had lived with the Nabateans since the destruction of the First Temple. Thus her family had been in constant contact with the Kenites, those people Father Moses had known so well and from whom he had chosen his wife, Zipporah. From the beginning of the story of Israel, the Kenites and the Jews had been in close touch with each other. It was these Kenites who had provided Judea with copper from the Wadi Aravah and who had taught the Jews how to make the fiery brass snake that Moses had put on his pole as a protection for his people.

Urzillah's father had been a caravan guide—one of the hundreds of men who earned their livelihood guiding caravans through every part of the known East. Like the hub of a large wheel, the Negev led out to the lands of Egypt, Syria, Edom, and even India. Urzillah's father carried all these routes on a map in his mind. From his father and his father's father before him, he had learned the geography of these vast lands. For this reason, his services were much sought after by all who were engaged in the commerce of the East. The wilderness of Shur, Wadi el Arish, Moab, Syria, Wadi Aravah, and the Mactesh Hagadol were as familiar to him as the streets of Arad.

He had never been rewarded with the rights of a citizen by the Nabateans; this was denied to Jews. Even the Idumeans could expect that right. Yet he was able to earn a good living that afforded them some comfort and even some small luxuries.

It was a disappointment to him that Urzillah was not a boy who could succeed him as caravan guide and carry on the tradition of his family. It was an even greater loss when his wife died in childbirth. But Urzillah traveled with her father as he carried the products of the lands—spices, balsam, frankincense, myrrh—to all parts of the East.

The camels that carried little Urzillah often bore, too, ivory bracelets, copper rings, mother-of-pearl pendants, and amulets, which would be sold in the markets of Damascus. Urzillah delighted in these ornaments and fine silks. For security she was dressed as a boy. To compensate for this masquerade, at the first opportunity she would dress in the frivolous garb and ornaments that women treasure. When a difficult and lengthy trip was over, she would clothe herself in India silk, filigree bracelets, and silver rings that her father gave her, and lavishly pour on herself the pungent perfumes of Arabia. Arrayed thus, she would play the flute for her enchanted parent.

The life of a caravaner was always dangerous, especially when torrential rains swept through the wadis with their flash floods. Nothing could stand up against the rushing waves, which would suddenly burst forth and race down the narrow canyons. A flood like this had carried her father away in front of her eyes.

That he had given his life for hers was quite evident. The torrent had come down on her left, and her father had moved, quickly behind her. When her mount stumbled, her father had pushed his own to her left to steady her against the flood of water, stones, and rocks coming down against her. In saving her, he himself had been swept away.

Her last glimpse of him, as he was carried away in a welter of baggage, animals, and rocks, was of his eyes, which carried a message of love and care for his daughter. She would see those eyes and feel their protecting love all her life.

It had happened so quickly, like all such tragedies of the desert, and it left Urzillah suddenly alone —except for Kenaz.

Kenaz was a caravan camel-driver whom Urzillah had known all her life. To him, who had loved his master and served him faithfully, Urzillah had entrusted herself, for there was no one else she could turn to. The caravaner and his daughter had never had a permanent home. Living among the gentiles, the father had avoided close associations that would have exposed Urzillah to closer contact with alien religions.

It had long been decided between them that both he and Urzillah would settle in a community that contained people of the Jewish faith when the opportunity presented itself. Fate had decided that the time for Urzillah was now. From Avdah in northern Nabatea, where the tragedy took place and where they had buried her father, she journeyed northward.

Leaving Avdah had been a common occurrence for Urzillah. This time, however, there was a finality about it. Now as they moved forward, the scenery changed from high cliffs and deep fissures to desert wastes, then to wide wadis in which the fields of barley and wheat were beginning to ripen. Oleanders and acacia bushes sprouted forlornly, while horned vipers, whose bite could bring horrible, writhing death, scurried at the caravan's approach. At times the wilderness was broken by the dull gray stones of the channels built by the Nabateans to divert the waters from the hills above them. The engineers had cleverly arranged the channels so that the porous earth would not absorb any of the precious water, thereby enabling the terraces below to receive the life-giving liquid from above.

The caravan had passed the city of Ain Hosb on the Wadi Aravah, where narrow catwalks marked the way through the hilly ranges. Only the legs of camels and mules were able to make their way along such narrow ledges.

Urzillah and her father had sometimes discussed the Jewish refuge on Masada. At various times it had been a Jewish community; at present it was the only Jewish center on this caravan route. Seated on her rocking camel, Urzillah spent the days dreaming of life on Masada, where she would for the first time be surrounded by people of her own heritage.

"If the gods will it!" The words came from her friend and protector as though he had looked into her mind.

The gods Kenaz referred to were those whose statues decorated the shrines that were to be found in the cisterns below the ground in his country—statues of Dushura or the god Zeus-Hadad, the mighty one of the thunderbolt. Kenaz accepted without question the religion of his people, the Kenites, as he did the life of a camel-driver with its daily hardships and dangers. Together with Urzillah's father, he had had the responsibility for the route of the caravan and the well-being of the beasts of burden. Salem, a Roman citizen, had been responsible for the financial arrangements of the caravan. The three had worked together, faithful employees of the owners who lived in comfort in Damascus and Alexandria while their caravan brought in its profits.

When Urzillah entered Masada, she stood before her hosts clad in a long Arab abaya. Her head was covered with a coarsely woven kefeya that hid her features and disguised her sex. Spontaneously, as she was accustomed to doing at the end of her desert journey, she threw off her headgear and reached for the pouch of engraved leather that hung at her side. From this she drew an ebony comb of great and delicate beauty and a little ivory mirror that had on its

reverse side the picture of the pagan goddess Ash-toroth, also called Astarte, who was known to the Greeks as Aphrodite and to the Romans as Venus, the goddess of love. The handle of the mirror formed the neck of the goddess, whose hair was piled in an elaborate coiffure covered with a conical cap.

That a Jewish girl should carry the image of the goddess seemed scarcely fitting, but a close observer would have noticed a resemblance between the proud, delicate beauty of the goddess and Urzillah, except that in the girl the arrogance was replaced by sweetness.

Urzilla had come a long way to throw her lot in with the defenders of Masada. With her she brought the spirit of youth and a cheerful nature. Masada was more than ever an ingathering of the exiles. It seemed as though every part of the known world was represented on this mountain.

But Urzillah was special; she who came from the parched desert exuded love—which in turn invited love.

6 / Come to the Fair!

As night was about to fall, the caravan of Kenaz drew up in the valley of Sebbeh. Salem approached the Roman camp, while Kenaz remained behind until negotiations were completed. They had arranged between them to try to convince the Roman commander to allow them to stay there and sell their goods. This would give them chance to make sure that the child of their friend had succeeded in reaching the top of Masada. A signal had been arranged for her to indicate that she was safe.

Salem was a shrewd trader and a man of the world. He was a Jew, born and raised in Rome. His father had been one of those Judean captives who had chosen to serve in Caesar's army. After his period of service, he and his children had been given the privilege of becoming Roman citizens. Latin was his native language. Now he succeeded in reaching the ear of the general and had obtained his permission. They could bring the caravan near the camp and carry on trade with the soldiers.

The arrival of a caravan bringing goods for sale was a welcome diversion for an army camped in a desolate region of the world. The officers, no less than the men, were eager for a change from the monotony of their days. The life of a soldier wavered between drudgery and danger. Unless some diversion was offered them in camp, the men would begin to quarrel among themselves.

The long march through the dull regions of rocky soil, and the speed Silva had set for the march, had strained the nerves of even the most experienced of the soldiers. Fights had erupted among the men over the bawdy camp followers. Men who were off duty passed the time in gambling and crude horseplay.

It was for this reason that General Silva was eager for the traders to stop at the Roman camp. He was willing to take a chance that there might be spies among the groups of traders who would pass on information to the enemies of Rome.

He had a particular distrust of Nabateans and Parthians, and both were in the caravan. The Nabateans were bold men who sailed their ships in the Mediterranean from Rhodes and Greece to Alexandria and Italy. The Roman command suspected that the Nabateans had, on occasion, helped the Jews in their fight against the Romans. As for the Parthians, the fact that they had never been conquered by the great armies of Rome rankled in the Roman mind. They lived on the banks of the Black Sea, secure in the knowledge that their armies could hold off the legions of Rome. And Silva knew that the Parthians were at this very moment negotiating with the Pharisees to come to the aid of the Jews against the Romans.

Well, let them try! thought Silva.

He smiled to himself. The future would have to take care of itself. In the meantime his troops merited a diversion.

It was certainly convenient to be a Roman citizen, Salem thought, as he walked away to spread the good news to the members of the caravan who waited for him in the valley. That is, he thought, with sardonic humor, if one had a lucky father who was destined to survive.

The following day the space in front of the military camp became the scene of great activity as the salesman set out their wares. There was beautiful pottery done in reddish brown with stylized floral and leaf patterns, using the palm and grape motifs. Some jars had beautiful rouletting, consisting of parallel lines with perforated dots or delicate crosslines. There was glass in delicate colors, rugs woven in India, silk from China dyed in the Tyrian purples of Phoenicia, pots of alabaster, ivory statuettes, buckles, bangles, necklaces, brooches, and pins of gold and bronze.

In another area, bags of grain formed the background for exotic foods of the East, fish from Spain, wine from Greece, dried fruits and honey—all tempting the appetites of soldiers tired of the unimaginative food served by the army kitchens.

The officers were the first to buy. The wily traders gave them preferential treatment to make sure the merchants would be allowed to stay for their main business with the common soldiers. Then the soldiers had their turn. The traders informed them that here was the opportunity to pick up choice goods of the East that would cost them much more in the marketplaces of the cities. Traditionally, a soldier's pay burns a hole in his pocket, and the traders did a brisk business.

"Perfume! Attar of roses!"

"Vases of ebony and gold and alabaster! Blue and yellow and red vases!"

"Come and get your charms here! Shells to keep off the evil eye!"

"Gods for your protection! Get your divine symbols!"

"Salve to ward off disease! Salve to clean wounds!"

"Myrrh and spices, pepper to pep up your appetites and to preserve your food!"

"Sandals and leather bags! Sandals decorated with papyrus!"

"Ribbons for the ladies!"

"Mirrors!"

"Kohl for your ladies' eyes!"

"Lapis lazuli!"

"Linens for your ladies! Shawls from the finest wools!"

"A libra of Greek cheese! Raisins! Olive oil!"

Money changed hands as the soldiers bought trinkets for their ladies at home or for themselves. A very popular booth was the one that offered beer made from barley bread. It quickly made the soldiers merry and added to the holiday atmosphere in the square.

The merchants had brought a magician to entertain the crowd. He sat on a carpet in front of a booth and twirled his colored balls.

"*Gulli gulli!*" he warbled in the hocus-pocus of the East.

The balls he juggled formed a rainbow around his head.

The smell of fragrant spices, cinnamon wood, and frying oriental food filled the air. The gruff voices of the men bargaining with the traders or tipsily singing bawdy soldier songs made a noisy background for this scene. The bleak encampment had turned into an animated, clamorous spectacle.

Into all this there floated down from the heights the thrilling notes of a distant flute.

Kenaz and Salem, walking on the outskirts of the circle of men and goods, heard the thin sweet notes of the delicate flute above the din of the market.

"Praised be the gods, or should I say her God," Kenaz said fervently. "She has been delivered to her friends. My promise to her father has been fulfilled."

7/ Mortar

For Eleazar ben Ya'ir, Huldah was always more than a mere aunt. She was a timeless symbol. For she maintained that she was determined to live to see the coming of the Messiah and great events in the history of the Jewish people. She said that she believed with perfect faith in the coming of the world of peace. Though that wonderful age had been postponed many times, she believed it would come and that she was destined to see it.

Her faith had carried her through the siege of Jerusalem and had brought her here to Masada. That trip to Masada was motivated by her conviction that Israel would be restored in her lifetime.

Eleazar was just as firmly convinced that this would happen, though he was more pessimistic regarding human mortality. But he was grateful to Huldah for her help in the past. He had known, in the days of the siege of Jerusalem, that he could trust Huldah with messages he needed to pass on to his men. He knew that Huldah would find a way to do it. Who would suspect an old woman of sabotage against the Romans? Eleazar knew, too, that he could always find a place in her home to rest and hide when the Romans were pursuing him after having set a price on his head. And knew that Huldah would always find something for his empty stomach.

Eleazar had not been surprised when Huldah found her way from Jerusalem to Masada. An old woman suffering with rheumatism, she had hobbled along the road in the Judean Desert, making slow progress, but finally arriving.

Once she was established in the fortress, Eleazar had given her the task of supervising the rations and the allotment of lodgings for the families of the community.

He knew that under her stern appearance there was a feeling heart and that she had an intuition for meeting people's needs and problems. He was sure that she would perform her duties with kindness, but would stand for no nonsense from those who might try to take advantage of her age.

Huldah accepted the assignment with one stipulation—that Eleazar would pass on her decisions before they were implemented so that he would be aware of the situation and back her up if any argument arose.

She had come to check with him in regard to the lodging that was to be given to Urzillah.

"If you don't mind, I will put Urzillah with Aviel's family. They have been here a long time and have a wonderful sense of family unity—something that Urzillah has not had. More than that—I think that young Aviel could learn from a stable young person like our young Nabatean."

Huldah loved the young and all the promise for Israel that they represented. She could never think of herself as being old. She felt rather pleased when she compared herself with Hannah, Yitzhak's grand-mother. Hannah, she thought, was both old and fussy.

"I agree," was Eleazar's reply.

Huldah continued, "Of course, you will have to give me a workman or two to get up a little partition between the family and Urzillah so that she can have some privacy. We should make some arrangement, too, for larger kitchen facilities since there will be more cooking needed in that apartment."

It was arranged that Yeshu would do the job, for he was the most experienced builder. The materials would be brought for him by Justus and Adin so that the work would be done quickly.

When the young men reported for work to Yeshu, they asked what materials he would need for con-struction. Yeshu said he would need only a quantity of stones of a smallish size, and plenty of clay and water. They could pick up all these materials in the open field, and the water could be brought from the cistern.

They worked busily with their spades, but Justus found time to talk. He was always interested in the life of the various countries of the Diaspora where Jews had settled. He asked Adin about Babylonia and the conditions there.

He himself came from a long line of Jews who had settled in Alexandria in the early days of the city. He had been brought up in completely assimilated conditions. The culture and society of Alexandria suited his life-style. Even his name, Justus, showed that he was more Alexandrian than Jewish.

As a result of his contacts with non-Jews, he had married a woman who was not of Jewish origin. Intermarriage was quite common in Alexandria, and the ceremony of converting the wife-to-be was done according to a familiar procedure. Sophia's name was changed to Sarah, and the rabbi introduced her to the blessings and taught her the dietary laws for the preparation of food.

"She did all this willingly because she loved me —though, of course, it did mean that she would be cut off from her family's religion. We were married according to the laws of Moses, and she, like Zipporah, Moses' wife, became a faithful wife and the mother of our children.

"Yet," he continued, "in the eyes of the Pharisees, she is not considered a Jewess. The Sadducees, who are governed only by the laws of the Bible, accept her; but the Pharisees dot every letter of their Talmud and have made life difficult for us. According to them, our children could not be accepted into the community. As far as they were concerned we were outcasts. This hurt my wife more than me. After all, she chose to come over to Judaism at great cost to herself. When the Romans turned on us and massacred the Jews, she proved her loyalty and fled with me here to Masada. Our children, alas, perished."

He fell silent, a prey to bitter memories.

Adin too was silent. After a while he said, "Unfortunately, this has always been a subject for much discussion and has even led to fighting between Jews. The Pharisees fear that Judaism will lose much of its meaning if outsiders are allowed in who are unfamiliar with our customs and ceremonies."

"I understand that," said Justus, "but I myself was not too familiar with them."

"Has her treatment been better here?" Adin asked.

"Yes, but it takes time for a woman with a bitter heart to forget the wrongs she has suffered in the past. The Sadducee rabbi who officiated at our wedding cautioned her that she would sometimes find that she would be challenged by those who were very scrupulous in their observance. I must admit, however, that here in Masada, differences seem to have been forgotten in the search for the common good. Besides, we are so busy that we forget politics and religious differences in our desire to survive."

"Yes," said Adin. "And there is always Eleazar ben Ya'ir to remind us that division will bring our downfall."

By this time they had filled the huge baskets with the clay and gravel.

Yeshu thanked them for the materials and asked them to stay and help with the plastering. The discussion continued as the three worked together.

"There is something that you have not talked about and perhaps we should consider it, too," Yeshu said in his gentle way. "You have not brought up the subject of the afterlife. For us Essenes, as for the Pharisees, this is very important. So here we have another principle that divides the Sadducees from other Jews."

As he worked with his trowel Yeshu continued. "We are bound to differ in our ideas about life and death. One man may say that the laws of the Bible are sufficient for him. Another man sees that there is need to interpret the Bible, which was given to the Jews so long ago. Still another Jew insists that he wants certain special ceremonies—we Essenes, for instance, insist on the laws of purity. Each man must follow his heart and find comfort in the ideas that appeal to him with the certainty that he is following the will of God. Unfortunately, when we do this, however, we break up into groups that disagree with each other and divide Israel."

Adin held out the mixture of mortar he had prepared for Yeshu.

"What will be the mortar that will hold us together as a people?" he asked. "What do we have as a people that will give us the will to work together and fight for our common good?"

It was Justus who found the answer.

"Perhaps we will realize at last that we must unite behind our leaders in time of national crisis. Perhaps we can forget the differences in ceremony and religious coloring. Perhaps we can adopt the idea that each man is entitled to his beliefs so long as he does not infringe on the beliefs of his neighbors."

"Amen!" was the fervent answer of Adin.

The sun began to sink behind the western mountain range. It was time for prayers. Each man on Masada would pray according to his own ritual. But while they prayed they kept watch. The enemy stood at the gates.

8 / The Ingathering of the Exiles

Aviel claimed that Urzillah belonged to his family. No, they hadn't adopted her, that was true. Huldah had brought her to the casemate apartment on the south side and had introduced her to the family. But she was to live with them so she could be looked upon as a relative.

"From Nabatea," Huldah had said.

"Where exactly is that?" was Aviel's question.

Urzillah told him about the Negev and described the life there. She told him about the mountainsides honeycombed with houses which had been dug out. She compared these houses to the cells built by busy bees, with a little opening for a door, just large enough to allow a person, stooped, to enter or leave. She said that only a sharp eye could distinguish the houses from the surrounding cliffs.

This made the town safer from enemy attacks. In addition, the houses were comfortable and eminently suited to the climate, since they allowed none of the outside heat to enter during the desert khamseen, nor the cold of the freezing mountains in winter.

She described to the fascinated listeners the town of Avdah, built on a plateau—a comfortable little town with plenty of wells and cisterns to supply fresh water for all their needs.

Later on, when Urzillah took her place with the women carrying water for the community of Masada, she told them of the cisterns of Avdah. There, in contrast to the cisterns of Masada, where you had to go down the stairs, she had dipped her jar into the water below by means of a rope, which was then drawn up. Rope marks scarring the stone casing of the well showed that the well had served the community for many centuries. Urzillah remembered how the depths of the cavernous walls had echoed with the voices of the girls who chatted and giggled as they drew water.

Urzillah was happy with her new life on Masada. Her father and she had often discussed the problems that would face a young person having to enter a community strange to her. At that time, the plan had been for both father and daughter to leave their wandering lives. Urzillah's father was getting older and he wanted to join his fellow Jews and end his days with people of his own faith.

"We are told that all Israel are brothers," he had said at the time. "But we have been scattered into the four corners of the world and have taken on the appearance and manners of the countries we have lived in.

"Actually, you may find less difficulty than others might, since you have traveled so much and have learned to get on with strangers. You have lived in a variety of places, each different from the other, and have learned to accept differences in people.

"Besides, I will be with you."

But all this had changed when he had given his life to save her. Fortunately, it was easy to love Urzillah. The people on Masada admired and respected the young girl who had braved the wilderness to come to them at this moment of decision. In time of common danger, people turn to each other for comfort and support. But Urzillah would have appealed to them at any time. She had the heart of a child and the knowledge of an adult who had suffered.

Indeed, to some she appeared to be a child and to others a woman. If Baruch, the young warrior, had been asked, he would have described her as a desirable woman. But Aviel and the children of the camp regarded her as one of themselves. Old Huldah, too, regarded her as a child.

Urzillah often confided in Huldah. She told her about her father and his contempt for the great ladies of Rome, for whom the perfumes, silks, and other exotic, expensive wares that he carried with such effort and in such danger were destined. Little did they worry—her father would say—about the men who died to supply them with the extravagances they accepted as a matter of course.

Huldah could remember such ladies when she thought of the ladies of Jerusalem. The wives of the Sadducees had had no need to stint themselves before the rebellion. They had lived lives of comfort, entertaining and being entertained by the Roman ladies with whose husbands their own husbands maintained business and government contacts.

The Pharisees, on the other hand, had refused social or business relations with the Romans, regarding such contacts as defilement.

"Here in Masada, my dear," said Huldah, "there are no rich and no poor. I give the same rations to each person, and we make sure that everyone gets what he needs."

She might have added, "And I sometimes give just a little more to the families who suffered in the long journey to Masada or in the siege of Jerusalem before that."

But she said no more and bent over her needle-work. She was working on a fine mantle for the Torah, fine enough to grace the Torah in the Temple that had been destroyed.

"How Father would have loved it here," Urzillah said. "How he would have loved to live among Jews!

"Yet he accepted his lot. But he wanted so much to remove me from the life of a caravan. He would say again and again, 'How much longer can you live the life of a wandering caravaner?' He said that it was about time that I should be wed."

Here she blushed a little.

Huldah caught the blush.

"Yes," she said, "with God's help, you will find someone who will make a good home for you so that you can live in the spirit of Sarah, Leah, Rebecca, and Rachel. I myself will live for the time when I can bring you to the wedding canopy and nurse your children as my own."

"Then my father will not have prayed in vain," was the answer. "Perhaps if the Pharisees are right and there is an afterlife, my father will look down from heaven and delight in my family. I shall give my child, my eldest boy, his name."

9/ Sicarii!

"Sicarii! Knife men! Assassins, murderers! Those are the names they have given us. And who drove us to these deeds? Who made us murderers?"

It was Eleazar talking to a work team who were dragging some of Herod's great stone columns to the parapets of the walls, ready to roll them down on attacking Roman forces.

As they prepared themselves for the Roman assault, the defenders engaged in wide-ranging discussions. It was as though the Zealots were attempting to examine their souls in preparation for the time when they would stand before the seat of the Almighty and there justify themselves and their actions.

"Who drove us to murder? For one hundred years we tried to live in peace with these Romans. For one hundred years we tried to find a way of putting up with Roman rule and Roman cruelty. We hoped to disregard their presence as long as they would let us observe our Torah. For one hundred years we tried to forget that the Romans were sucking our country dry. The beautiful Galilee, with its wheat fields and its great green forests, was being turned into a wilderness where two blades of grass could not grow. Before the coming of the Kittim, the Galilee was a land of palms and figs, of olives and honey, of pastures and of lakes teeming with fish."

Nachum and Baruch were both Galileans. Rome had always considered the word Galilean to be synonymous with rebel, without considering why it was that patriotic feeling was always being aroused in northern Israel. Eleazar's words struck them forcibly, and they pushed more vigorously at their section of the pillar, translating their anger into action.

Eleazar spoke in the name of all Israel.

"We tried to forget the cries of our brothers broken on the torture wheel. We bent our backs and paid the procurators the last of our coins. The money went into the pockets of the procurators Herod, Antipater, Florus, and Cestus, who gorged themselves on the blood of our land and our people.

"And what money did reach Rome was spent on those siege machines below, which destroy our cities, or used to build the roads over which their soldiers march to kill us. The cleverest of engineers are employed to cut through the rocks and mountains to bring soldiers to repress Jews who have dared to question the justice of Rome. We, who only wanted to live in peace in our land, have paid for the swords on which they, the Romans, impale our babies who dare to cry for milk or for their mothers, who have been sent off to slavery.

"So we carried the dagger—the *sica*—and we carried it in our clothing, hidden so that we could better surprise the tyrants who had come to suck our lifeblood.

"There are those among us who said, 'Peace, peace. Peace at any price!' For this we must thank the Sadducees."

Eleazar pronounced the name with extreme bitterness.

"The Sadducees were willing to pay any price for the privilege of worshiping in the Holy Temple. Well, the price they finally paid was the Temple itself.

"And when Florus, cursed be his name, brought the Roman eagle into the Temple, when he seized the vestments of the high priest and made himself guardian of those holy vestments, and put them in the Antonius Tower, which flanks the Temple area, then even the Sadducees saw that their policy of peace, peace, was one of shame, shame.

"Florus! Greed itself! Seventeen golden talents had to be paid out of the Temple funds before the Levites could garb themselves to serve the Lord at the Passover festival. Even the men of peace could be silent no longer. Then they were happy to be called Sicarii like ourselves.

"How the Romans must have laughed as they watched from the Antonius Tower and saw Jew fighting Jew.

"So we burned the Office of Records in the palace of Berenice and destroyed all the records and deeds. Let them now find out who owed money to the Roman coffers.

"Yes, we are Sicarii, the war party. Where were the men of peace, our brethren, at the time when we could have driven the Romans from the Holy Temple? Why did they not see the justice of our cause then?"

Justus slowly straightened as Eleazar continued his enumeration of Roman acts of oppression.

"When the Jews of Caesaria, twenty thousand in number, were attacked in cold blood without any warning, they stood shoulder to shoulder. They died, but they died with dignity. So, too, the Jews of Alexandria—fifty thousand of them who had lived in the city founded by King Alexander, honored by the people of the world for their culture and learning. The Jews helped to build Alexandria when the ancestors of Florus were still living in caves as unwashed barbarians. Our people lived in Damascus, Tyre, Hilpos, Machaerus, and many other cities; in all of them the blood of our Jewish brethren ran in the streets, the blood of our beloved brothers."

And of our little children, Justus thought sadly.

"Oh, they did not die like dogs—they fought like lions. In all the cities of the Decapolis they rose and resisted the Roman tyrants, and they died fighting like men.

"Before my eyes I can still see Simon ben Giora, he of the brave heart; Simon, knowing that Jerusalem was lost, escaping through the sewers of Jerusalem in the hope of making his stand here in Masada with us. Simon, caught by the Romans and dragged in a noose through the streets of Rome to the Forum, where he was lashed to death. Simon, the beautiful, who knew no fear, who had leaped out from the battlements, mounted a Roman siege tower, and attacked its builders; Simon, who forced the Romans to flee and who brought back a war machine for us to use against the Romans; Simon, who then gave the retreating Romans such a severe beating that they left their baggage animals and war contraptions behind them; the Tenth Legion, the pride of Vespasian, shamed; Simon, who took Hebron from the Romans and brought its corn and food to the starving little ones of Jerusalem."

Nathaniel marveled at his chief. He had never allowed himself the luxury of tears when Simon had been killed, or when his own family was wiped out in the bloody wars against the empire.

Eleazar continued dispassionately, as though reciting a history lesson.

"Simon was a Sicarius, and proud of the name. He was treated as an ordinary criminal, instead of being shown the courtesy due a brave and honorable fighter.

"They were afraid of us, these Romans, so afraid that Vespasian took his favorite, the Tenth Legion, out of the siege of Jerusalem and put in Arabs and Syrians instead. He did not care if those mercenaries lost their lives. He wanted only to save his Tenth Legion.

"At Jerusalem we burrowed under the walls and pushed burning wood under the siege towers, so that the towers toppled and fell back on the Romans. We considered this a partial payment for the four thousand Jews whom they had once chased through the narrow streets of the Jerusalem marketplace, and then murdered or dragged out of their houses to be scourged and flayed with metal whips and then crucified.

"And why? Because they had dared to question the taxes they had to pay. Because they dared to dramatize their feelings by pretending to beg at street corners for 'poor Florus' who had so little money and needed so much."

Nathaniel remembered how his father had come home from the market and how he had laughed at this ridiculous scene. A beggar stood on every corner bearing a cup for "poor Florus."

Eleazar continued his recapitulation of the history of the wrongs which the Jews had suffered.

"How Agrippa, of the family of the Hasmoneans, implored the Sicarii to give in; how he offered them a place in his army if they would surrender and lay down their arms! Josephus, too, made his speeches, standing alongside Vespasian, advising us to surrender. What was ben Giora's answer? 'It is better to be destroyed at once rather than by degrees. For what value is a Roman's promise?' Yes, what trust can be placed in the promise of a Roman? We would have been taken to the Colosseum to fight with wild beasts just like the rest of the captives.

"We have learned many things in our wars. We have learned that when God wills it, we must fight. What day? It doesn't matter—Sabbath, Succoth, Passover! Where shall we fight? Where the enemy is, there we must fight. This lesson was taught to us by the greatest of them all—Mattathias, father of the Maccabees. This was taught to us by Menachem, of blessed memory.

"When the walls of Jerusalem were breached by the thousands of war machines, it was with their bodies that our Sicarii defended the Holy City. Even when the wall was breached, there were still brave men who made sorties out of the city. When we were short of water at Machaerus, we hung wet garments soaked in water on the battlements to fool the enemy into thinking that we had plenty of water. We held out against their towers, which were so tall that they were able to see us within our walls.

"We were men then, as now, but we ourselves gave Titus the victory. For we were divided in our politics. Pharisees, Sadducees—we could not agree between us. Whether to allow the Romans to stay in our country; whether to learn to live with them; whether to allow people like Herod to sacrifice in the Holy Temple—we could not agree. We could not agree. We gave the enemy our city. We should have met the Romans together as one man. We should have been united in our purpose."

The man was tireless.

"Let this thing not happen here on Masada. We have people with us of all political opinions. But we are united in our stand. We hate the Romans and what they represent. Here, too, our people hate blood. What Jew does not abhor the idea of shedding blood? There are those with us—the Essenes—who live in strict accordance with the law of the prophets, pure in body and pure in soul, who have devoted their lives to cleanliness and to purity. We even have with us men who have accepted the principles of Jesus.

"Pharisees, Sadducees, Essenes, Christians—to-day we are all Sicarii. We will live by the sword, and, if it be the will of God, we will die by the sword. But we will drive the Romans from our land.

"There will be no God but the Almighty, blessed be His name. There will be no tax but the Temple tax. There will be no friends but the Zealots, those who are zealous for the Lord. With these will we stand against the foreign invaders."

The men worked mightily while they spoke. Eleazar's words drove them and drove him, too.

10 / The New Moon

"It's a boy! May he live to one hundred and twenty like Moses, our father and teacher! May he be privileged to see Zion restored! May he see Jerusalem rebuilt!"

The news spread through the camp, and the joy of the Zealots knew no bounds. The beginning of a new life seemed to be an omen for the success of their cause and that of the Jewish people. It renewed their hope and confidence.

Ohada had worked until the labor pains overtook her, and then the little baby who belonged to her and to Adin had come. Little Yehudah, who had endured the privations of the desert while he was being carried by his mother, had come quickly, like a true pioneer. His entrance into the world seemed easy, as though the baby already carried the instinct to be helpful so that his mother could carry on her share of the work. She had helped in the important tasks of insuring the supply of water to the camp.

The month of Adar brought hot weather. The task of providing water from the great underground cisterns was given to the women and children. They worked very hard to bring water from the cisterns to the top of the mountain.

As the time of Ohada's delivery approached, the women suggested that she stop her activities. But

Ohada refused. It was hard work descending the long steep steps of damp stone that led down into the cistern. The cisterns were huge cavernous chambers hollowed out at Herod's command into the bowels of the earth and supported by huge pillars. The walls were covered with white plaster that prevented the water from being absorbed into the ground. An aqueduct carried the rainwater into the cistern. Several years' supply of water for the community was stored in these cisterns.

The white columns and walls reflected the dim light. when water was low, the water-carriers had to descend even farther down. There was no rail on the steps, and the women had to feel their way in the semidarkness. The return trip with the full jar of water balanced on their heads was very precarious. It took a great deal of skill and patience to reach the top, where the older women took the jars and stored them in a row from which the individual families could take their rations.

Later, at the suggestion of the governing council of the camp, the drawing of the water was done at night when the heat of the day was past. Then huge torches were fitted into the niches on the pillars, giving the cave a beautiful otherworldly air as the light shimmered on the tranquil surface of the pool. At this hour, there was a feeling of mystery that was intensified by the remoteness of the hilltop. The workers felt the challenge in the task that called for a sense of courage.

When she felt stronger, Ohada resumed her place in the line of water-carriers and left Yehudah in the care of one of the older women.

Little Yehudah bar Adin had come into the world on a Sabbath day, and so he was circumcised on the following Sabbath. In the synagogue the father handed the boy to Eleazar, who, acting as godfather, then handed Yehudah to the mohel who performed the rite. The name given him was repeated in a clear voice, announcing his entrance into the fold of his people.

The stillness of the Sabbath spread its mantle over the camp and was in sharp contrast to the noise and activity of the Roman positions. That night Silva, in anticipation of the siege and to keep up the morale of his troops, called on all ranks for a full-dress parade. Drums sounded. Gleaming brasses and polished blades reflected the fire from the flickering torches. Each unit was headed by its standard.

From the battlements above, the shofars sounded a shrill alarm. The Jews rushed to their positions. On the hill, facing the main Roman camp, they saw what Silva hoped would strike fear into their hearts.

In full view of the enemy, Silva mounted a dais and signaled the trumpets to sound again. The assembled legionaries stood at strict attention.

Silva proclaimed, "I make you a promise that before the summer is over, we will have driven this band of rebels to surrender. We have only to complete the road up the cliff and the fortress is ours. Our engineers tell me that the job will take no longer than two weeks. You have done well. The battle will be brief. The blacksmiths are busy at their fires putting your arms in top condition. Your arrows will be swift and sharp. See to it that your swords and the points of your spears are keen. We will show these barbarians how

Roman metal can 'cure' those who dare to taunt Rome."

The troops received his words with enthusiasm, clashing their swords against their shields and shouting for victory.

Silva had intended by this assembly to frighten the Jews. But the words were lost in the darkness to the people on the hill. In the silence that followed, the Romans heard the confident chant of a multitude of voices in prayer. As the wedge of the crescent moon showed itself in the sky, the Jews assembled on the side of the cliff facing the Roman camp and began to perform the service of blessing the new moon. Shoulder to shoulder they prayed and danced, their feet beating out the rhythm of the chant.

Even the sombre Essenes, whose ritual was more dignified and who stood with their prayer shawls covering their heads in recognition of the awesomeness of God, did not disapprove of this scene of joy and near frivolity.

The ritual continued according to its ancient form.

"As I dance before You and cannot touch You, so may my enemies not touch me and not reach me for evil.

"May fear fall upon them at the sight of the strength of Your arm. May their strength sink as a stone into the depths of the water."

The circle beat out the joyful prayer.

"A good sign, a sign of good luck, shall be upon me and upon all Israel. Peace unto You, living God of Israel."

11 / The Last Days

A Roman taunted him from below.

"Don't fall off the wall, little soldier. You may hurt yourself on the little stones if you do."

Adin was standing guard on the walls. His instructions were to patrol his sector of the walls, to observe any Roman military activity, and to look out for spies who might make their way into the camp or sabotage any of the defense.

There was now no longer any possibility that others would come to join those already at Masada. Leaving was equally difficult. The whole area was crowded with workers; in addition, Roman guards were posted along the periphery. Encircling the rock, work parties involving every soldier were setting up the eight camps that would house the legionaries. The Tenth Legion was to take the most important of these sites—the camp on the west side near the path and commanding the view of the northern palace, and the one on the east facing the Snake Path and the eastern side of the rock.

Joining these camps, roads were being laid—one leading east and west, the headquarters' road, and the other north and south, the troop commander's. A Roman guard, Adin's counterpart, was standing in the front gate behind which an added wall was being built for greater security for the command post. The two roads would cross each other in the center of the four gates.

Around him, men toiled with pick and saw, leveling the ground. The stones were being saved in piles for the erection of the tent foundations and for the beds that would be made for each man. The tent covering would be of canvas, with poles to hold down the ends.

A command post was being made by workmen—somewhat more comfortable than that for the common soldier. These posts were placed in open square formation and could accommodate twelve officers. Their mess centers were more elaborate than that for the men.

Near the quarters for the officers, a dais was being erected for the general to address and review his troops. There were also administration buildings, a marketplace, and other offices.

Close by were the altars for sacrifices and an observatory from which the flights of birds would be observed, as omens to show whether the gods favored the attack.

The work went forward in all haste, for there was still the giant circumvallation to be built before the attack was sprung. Huge cranes were preparing the large rocks that would be used for this great wall.

Adin's eyes took in the activity and saw the planning and order behind this huge undertaking. He had mixed feelings about guard duty. True, it gave you a chance to think and evaluate your whole attitude—to carry on a two-way dialogue with yourself and to come to a conclusion as to how you felt about life and its problems. Then you could sort out the different ideas being aired in the meetings you had with the people of Masada. A person had to know how he felt about things.

But duty on the walls also exposed you to the taunts and scorn of the Roman soldiers and their crude manners.

Well, it would be wisest to pay no attention. Your eyes could still search out the surrounding area, while your mind could think and come to conclusions.

Was this indeed the end of days foretold by the Essenes? Were the forces of darkness to win over the world, as the prophet had said? Would the Messiah then come when life was at its worst? Would all the world crumble and the kingdom of God begin?

It might as well, thought Adin. Everything has become so difficult, so involved. Gone are the days of Abraham and the peaceful simple life of those shepherds of Canaan.

It was more than the human mind could disentangle. Perhaps a person should stop trying to stand up against the dark strength of Rome and the violence she represented. Let her conquer and let the end of days come so that the Messiah and his reign could begin. Since we hope for the Messiah and the kingdom of God, why bother opposing the forces of evil? Let them roll over the world and let the messenger of peace take dominion after that.

This Messiah—who was he?

There were some who said that the man Jesus had been this messenger. Yet, though thousands had flocked to his teachings, there was still no sign of peace. On the contrary, conditions had worsened. The Jews who had become Christians had been persecuted by Rome no less than other Jews. Both Jews and Christians had been sent to Rome in chains to fight the wild beasts in the arena. Both Jews and Christians had lost their lives in the Colosseum or on the cross. The Romans used any excuse to send them to their death. Any outrages that occurred were immediately blamed on the Jews. The latest scandal was when Nero blamed the Jews for the fire that destroyed Rome—though everyone knew that Nero himself had started the fire. If you were trying to find an easier life than that of a Jew, it would not be that of a Christian.

Become a Christian? How could a believing Jew agree that a man born of woman was God? And what of the other claims made for Jesus? That he was born of the tribe of Benjamin and not of the priestly Levites seemed unimportant. Nor was it important that it was claimed that Jesus was of the family of Melchizedek, who, long before Levi, had been the priest who had blessed Abraham.

Other signs had been sought to prove that Christ was the Messiah of the Jews: he had come into Jerusalem riding on a donkey, a star had shown to foretell his coming—all these signs seemed to be mere legends told by men to magnify the importance of a leader. For indeed Jesus had become a gigantic figure to those new Christians, though barely fifty years had passed since his death.

Adin paced up and down the wall.

What was to be done? Should one become passive and allow tyrants to have their own way? The men of

Ein Gedi had stopped fighting and had opened the gates to the Romans, deciding that further opposition was futile. Should one give in—or was this a time when a man had to stand up for the principles in which he believed?

Adin longed to reach out with his hands and throttle each of the human ants toiling below. But there was no use wasting your energy in hate. Adin could only watch and wait. It was better to keep working, making preparations, storing stones and arrows and flammable torches for the defense.

From now on the only thing to do was to watch every move of the Romans and try to defeat their plans.

Adin tried to think back into the past. Why had Judea always been the battleground for the wars of the Egyptians, Babylonians, Persians, Greeks, and Romans?

Why should a Jew choose *Pax Romana?* Perhaps if he did it would insure the Jews the safety due an ally of Rome. With powerful Rome defending Judea, perhaps a person could go on with his business while the Romans did the fighting. Then the Jew would be safe.

Safe? Safe for what? To pay the huge taxes that squeezed the very life from everyone—farmer, shepherd, and artisan? How safe could one be when the very tithe of the Temple was stolen from the treasury in the Temple? Surely any man worthy of being called a man must rise against such atrocities.

Adin recalled that there was now living on Masada a man who had come all the way from Rome to join the patriots. He told of Jews who lived in Rome and enjoyed the rights of full citizenship. They worshiped in their own synagogues and were exempt from the exorbitant taxes which noncitizens had to pay. Why not strive for this? Josephus himself, the writer and former Jewish general who had turned traitor, was now in Rome, enjoying all the rights of Roman citizenship. The only duty expected of him was that he write books about the benefits of being a good and obedient Roman.

What made people like Eleazar and his uncle Menachem before him throw away comfort and lead difficult and dangerous lives? Diehards? There were 960 such diehards behind the walls of Masada.

Adin's thoughts were disturbed by the noise of someone shouting again, "Little soldier, little soldier!"

There was the Roman guard making derisive gestures just out of bowshot. The words accompanying the gestures were in Aramaic and were the coarsest insults in the filthy vocabulary of a common soldier. Probably the man was a Syrian mercenary. Certainly he had spent some time in the Middle East.

Adin averted his gaze from the coarse face of the Roman. He pretended that he had not heard. The last words were the most nauseating of all. The Roman was using the vilest words for the Jewish family and Jewish women. It was hard to suffer all this, and to divert his thoughts Adin looked along the walls.

What a good thing, he reflected, that Herod built the fortress so strong.

Herod had thought he would have to use it against Cleopatra, who had wanted his position as governor. However, with Herod's usual luck, he was able to bribe his superiors, the Roman officials, who had then allowed him to remain as procurator.

Herod! Herod again! It was as though Herod epitomized what Adin was fighting against. A man born of an Idumean (Edomite) father who had become Jewish and who was considered a Jew—a Jew about whom the Law said: "Thou shalt not hate the Edomite in your heart." The Edomites were considered the newest of all Jews, because they had been the last to embrace Judaism. They had been brought into the Jewish fold by the Maccabees, who had reclaimed the Negev for Israel.

Herod! He was considered by some to be the Messiah who would bring peace into the world. A man who loved beauty, who had rebuilt the Temple in Jerusalem with granite blocks even bigger and more impressive than those in the Temple built by King Solomon. He had added to the wall of the Second Temple the beautiful towers that had been strong enough to withstand the latest Roman siege.

So many Messiahs, thought Adin. It seemed that men were always looking for the kingdom of heaven and grasping at any straw to find peace. When a man can no longer find hope on earth, he hopes that salvation will come from above.

The Jewish religion, Adin thought, was founded on one commandment above all: I am the Lord, thy God; thou shalt have no other God before Me. So how could one believe that Herod or anyone else who had already appeared could be the God-given Messiah? Certainly the Messiah could not be Herod, who had been willing to bow down to both the Roman eagle and to God.

Adin thought he had found the answer. Masada would stand against the Romans, just as the Jewish idea of God would stand against the idolatry of the Romans.

He shifted his feet, which had grown weary of standing, and moved his hand down the wooden shaft of his spear. The watch was becoming tiresome and he was anxious to do something more active.

As though in answer to his impatience, the Roman guard called again. "Now, now, now, little soldier, do you think your God will be of any help to you?"

The guffaw which accompanied the words showed plainly the contempt the Romans had for the people who believed in an unseen God.

Adin once again decided not to reply to the Roman's scorn. At this moment he reminded himself of a Persian proverb he had learned in the city of Babylon: "A word is a bird. Once it is released, no one can capture it."

He stared into the valley without uttering a word.

Adin was glad when Etan, his relief, turned up. Etan was a young man who had spent some time in Rome before coming to join the Zealots in Masada. He understood the Romans. He could get back at the Roman guard and give him argument for argument in the battle of words across the wadi.

But words would soon no longer be the only weapons used in the valley of Sebbeh.

12 / Iddo Helps

Iddo liked to feel that he was important to the defense of Masada even though he was only eleven years old. Each day when his mother excused him after the chores had been done, he would report to the headquarters of Eleazar. He carried messages to and from the command post or lugged arrows and other war materials from the artisans who manufactured them to those who would be using the materials when the time came.

Even though he was not yet a man, Iddo had few illusions about war. He remembered only too well the siege of Jerusalem, which took place when he was seven years old. The horror of that time remained with him still. He had a good idea of what lay ahead of him.

But when Iddo was with Eleazar and his officers, all fear vanished. They seemed to have a feeling of confidence about them; sometimes they even told a funny story. This was very reassuring to a child who had memories of terror and flight and hunger and cold.

Eleazar looked up from the papyrus on which he had been writing with a stylus.

"Iddo, it's you. Be a good lad and find Nathaniel

for me. He can't be far. I have to lie down for a while, and Nathaniel should know that he is in charge."

He yawned wearily.

"In fact, I'll lie down this minute because I know that I can depend on you to get him. If you can't find him, wake me."

Certainly a commander such as Eleazar would not leave his post until his substitute came. He wanted Iddo to feel important. Nathaniel was close by —in fact he was supervising the production of armor scales being made in the garrison building just behind the administration building. The Romans had left a huge oven now being used by the Zealots to melt down metallic objects. The molten iron was poured into molds shaped like large scales. While the metal was still red hot, four holes were punched with a metal rod. Then the scales could be strung on a lining of leather to turn aside the point of an arrow or spear.

The men toiled over the hot charcoal fire into which pitch from the Asphalt Sea had been poured to increase the heat. The sweat ran down the faces and bodies of the men. Nathaniel was wringing wet.

He gave instructions for the men to continue and for the scales already completed to be delivered to the women working on the garments in the casemate sections of the wall; then he hurried back to headquarters with Iddo at his side.

"Lucky thing we got a good supply of scales when we took over the fort." he said. "You should have seen the expressions on the faces of the Romans the day we entered this building. Their eyes were bulging in surprise. It was just the time when things were beginning to go wrong for us in the Galilee, when Josephus,

son of Matthew, was beginning to talk about surrender. Some of us had the feeling that this Josephus
was not the brave hero we had thought him to be. He
was, when we came to think about it, the one who
always found himself in a safe place when others
faced death.

"The day we captured Masada we climbed quietly up the north side. The Romans did not dream
that we were anywhere near the place, and their
watch was slack. I laugh every time I think about it.
There were not many of them, for no one thought that
Masada was important at the time. Everyone thought
that Jerusalem and the Galilee would win the war for
the Romans and that would be the end."

Nathaniel went on. "We found a good supply of
everything. These Romans don't stint themselves on
supplies. That was one time when we got some re-
turns for our taxes."

Nathaniel chuckled. "And bows and arrows and
knives and shields. Thank God for the Roman Empire
and their supplies. And their workmanship is splen-
did."

Then he became serious.

"With God's help we will use these weapons
against them to good purpose."

"Amen!" was Iddo's answer.

Like Eleazar, Nathaniel made a person feel that
there was work to be done. He made a person feel
important.

"Can you stay or will you be needed at home?"
Nathaniel asked gravely. "I can always use a good
man like you."

"I can stay," said Iddo.

Then he said, reverting back to their earlier subject, "Was it really that easy to take Masada?"

"In war," said Nathaniel, "you must always be on your guard. And for once the Roman guard was down, thinking that we were done for in the Galilee. They thought that Vespasian had gotten rid of us for all time and that all the Jews would be killed or would surrender there. What was it Vespasian once said? 'The only good Jew is a dead Jew.' But he couldn't get rid of us so easily. Even when he burned Jerusalem, some of our men were able to escape by means of the tunnels under the city."

A person could always learn from Nathaniel. He made you feel like an adult.

They returned to the room where Eleazar lay on his cot. Nathaniel was surprised to see him there. But Eleazar signaled him with a quick wink, and Nathaniel saw that the commander wished to build Iddo's self-confidence. Then Eleazar grunted and turned over, away from the light. For a moment his eyes had opened and registered what was there; now he was asleep. Eleazar was not the kind of man to be caught napping—even literally.

Nathaniel looked into the cupboard on the wall. It was empty.

"You could help us with our rations," he said. "We haven't had our meal today and could do with some of the oil and dates they have."

He gave Iddo three copper coins that fuctioned as ration tokens. Iddo took a basket and jar from the cupboard. He knew that he must also get the bread for the day.

A short walk brought him to the warehouse near

the west gate in the wall. Huldah was on duty there, and from her seat in the doorway she was able to supervise the entire rationing system.

How cool and pleasant it was in the warehouse! That was because all the rooms were long and faced north. No wonder the food was always so fresh and good to eat! The walls were made of stones as thick as they were wide. Iddo could visualize the immense Roman machines that had raised these stones, which had probably been cut on the south side of the fortress.

What a wealth of supplies! Iddo wondered at the quantity. Though it was carefully rationed, Iddo knew that there was enough for all for a very long time. There was oil and wine and dried fish, each kind of staple in its own kind of jar.

Before he left with the supplies, Iddo looked into the special room where the Temple offerings were kept. There were the jars marked with the words MA'ASSER KOHEN. This was the tithe put aside by everyone for the Temple priests according to the Law of Moses. Since the priests were allotted no portion in the land, the rest of Israel had to provide for them.

Will we have Jerusalem again? Will the Temple be rebuilt? Iddo wondered. Then he shook his head. That's not the way to think about it. I'll try again. When we rebuild the Temple, we will take the Temple offerings with us to Jerusalem.

He lingered to smell the herbs and dried fruitcakes of dates and figs and dried grapes. It reminded him of the stories his parents told about the beauty and fertility of the land of Israel.

"A land flowing with milk and honey," they would say with pride.

Saying good-bye to Huldah, Iddo carried his basket and jar back to Nathaniel. Then he went to the west casemate near the southern tip where the bakehouses were. He smelled the warm bread just out of the oven, baked from wheat that was actually raised behind the western palace on this very mountaintop. Between the palace and the southern wall, a piece of ground had also been plowed and planted with vegetables.

Miriam, Aviel's mother, was in charge of the ovens. She removed some warm flat bread from an open oven and gave Iddo several loaves in exchange for the token he handed her, plus a piece for himself to nibble on as he went back with the provisions.

Iddo walked by the casemate rooms far down on the west side, where hides were hanging on the walls of one of the chambers. This was the home of the leather-worker. He was concentrating on making leather vests, which would be covered with metal scales to protect the fighting men of Masada. Even the women would wear them while bringing food and arms to the warriors.

Other members of the community were working on the shields, which, Roman fashion, were made of leather stretched over frames of wood and were held with a metal handle that the soldier could slip over his left hand, leaving his right hand to hold his weapon.

Iddo was tempted to walk back by way of the southern casemate apartments. He could see the women entering the tower on the south, carrying

with them the jars they would fill in the cisterns on the south side. This was indeed a busy tower, leading as it did to some of the casemate rooms on the southern tip and to the caves, which were being used by some of the families.

Iddo had once teased his mother into letting him sleep with a family in one of the caves on the south wall. It seemed such a good adventure. But he had to admit to himself afterward that though living in a cave sounded like fun, it really wasn't as comfortable as living in a casemate room on the wall. Casemates were crowded, but at least the floor was level and you did not have to go about stooped to keep from banging your head.

The more people there were in Masada, the more crowded it was—but that made its defense surer. Iddo silently blessed the newcomers.

His tasks had been completed, and Eleazar and Nathaniel would be able to eat for a while. Iddo felt content.

He, too, had a share in the defense of the Rock.

13 / Rome Is Impatient

A runner stood before Silva. Slates, hinged together, hung from his neck. A message had been written on the inner side, and the slates then placed face to face and tied with a string, which in turn had been closed with a big lump of wax on which the great seal of the emperor had been imprinted.

The general eyed the man, admiring the physical perfection of the Greek. He was built for the purpose —lithe, without an extra ounce of fat, and long of leg. His leg muscles stood out like the bulges on a knotty pine tree.

These legs had covered many hundreds of miles of Roman roads. Broad shoulders and a large chest made breathing an effortless task. Surely this must be a descendant of those Greeks who had carried the messages of the Greek generals in the days of their empire. Selective breeding had developed a human machine designed for this one purpose.

The messenger stood in the triangular opening of the tent, his breathing quickened a little from the climb into camp, although his run over the rest of the road had made few demands on him.

"Sire!"

The runner had been well schooled in the proper way of addressing his superiors.

"Speak!"

"Sire, I have been asked to make no delay in bringing your answer. I have been ordered to begin my return journey to the emperor within the hour."

Silva broke the seal, removed the string, and scanned the message.

"It is well," was his answer to the runner. "You shall have your reply within the hour. You may take the opportunity to attend to your needs. If you so desire, you may refresh yourself at my cook's kitchen. Perhaps a drink of honey and wine would be refreshing to your parched throat."

There was a hint of amusement in Silva's manner; he seemed to be enjoying a private joke. In fact he was mentally thumbing his nose at the powers that were constantly nagging him about his job. He patted the short hair over his forehead and regarded something in the distance as the runner departed.

The Greek was scarcely out of hearing when Silva broke up in laughter, much to the bewilderment of his aide-de-camp. When his merriment finally ceased, Silva explained its cause to Demetrius. The emperor was becoming restless with the Judean campaign and was anxious to close the affair. Titus was fearful that the world would discover that the coins he had minted were telling a lie.

"Judaea capta" they read, whereas in point of fact, the land of the Jews had only been partly captured. Witness to this was the fact that the Romans had their army in all its strength camped here, trying to put down a people who supposedly had ceased to exist. A group of diehards in the middle of a desolate desert on a huge rock were making the mighty Roman Empire look ridiculous.

Silva had been quite prepared for the contents of the slate. He could have recited the stilted, formal language of the military message without looking down to read it.

"Hail, Silva, procurator of Judea, proud ambassador of Pax Romana! We salute you in the name of the gods of Rome. No signal has as yet arrived from you proclaiming your victory over the stiff-necked villagers of Palestine. We would welcome knowledge of what has been accomplished. The people of Rome are anxious to prepare the great libations to our gods and to celebrate the victory of the eagle in the Palestinian outposts of the Roman Empire."

Silva was amused. His great laugh rang out again. Demetrius was afraid that the messenger was within earshot.

"Bah! They sit at their desks and try to tell me how to fight their battles. Or dally with their slave girls from the marketplace. Or listen to their slaves playing their lyres. Or go to the circus to watch the fights between men and wild beasts. They feast their eyes on the blood of men in the Colosseum while we watch our men shed their blood in battle. And while we sweat here in the desert heat, they gorge themselves with food, reclining on their couches, proud of the quantity of food they can put down their gullets. They can find nothing else to do but make plots against one another—and when necessary, murder each other for position and power. While I—I slave for the empire. One year of preparation—months of marching through the deserts and mountains, suffering thirst and weariness, weakened by disease, building towers and platforms and drawbridges, preparing great timbers for the rams and the towers and the ladders, getting and hauling pitch, making the swords, the bows and arrows, and the spears, fighting the floods, finding the toughest fighters I could get, traveling to the farthest corners of the Roman Sea—to Delos, to the Balearic Islands off Spain—to get men to follow me who will stop at nothing, men who will face death without fear, who will follow the standard of Rome without question, for the empire. All this Silva does, while they play their flutes and their fiddles and plan their intrigues."

Demetrius knew. He had had to keep up with his chief, who worked as though he was possessed by a demon.

"And the enemy we face here—like the Britons and the Gauls who fought us, but even worse, for these men are fanatics: Jews who will go to their death singing to their God. We saw them at Jerusalem. How they tricked us—they burrowed under the city and under our very towers to set fire to them. They captured our stores and handed out the food and the arms to their own people.

"To fight these people at Masada is more difficult than the task of Vespasian was at Jerusalem. Eleazar ben Ya'ir has been a fighter since his youth. His men have watched us and learned our methods. They have turned our tactics against us. From the Galilee, from Jerusalem, from Alexandria and Ein Gedi, they bring their hatred and their determination to get rid of us."

Demetrius ventured to sit down, choosing the most comfortable chair available. He knew that this speech would take some time. His chief was just getting warmed up. From this long speech, Silva would develop his next step in this battle of wits with the emperor.

Silva continued.

"We fight according to plan. We use the tactics we have learned from our books on the science of war, and from our masters, the generals who came before us. These men in front of us fight with an agile brain in unexpected ways. They are quick to learn. They are intelligent. They know their land like the palms of their hands. They could, I imagine, find their way through this wilderness blindfolded.

"We are fighting a determined people and we fight them on their own ground, yet the emperor writes: 'When can we expect to hear of the victory of the eagle?'

"Bah! Let them come and try their hand at it. We would soon see how quickly they could put down this rebellion."

Demetrius spoke up from where he sat poised on the camp chair. "But, sire, the letter! You promised to give the runner his answer within the hour."

The general reached into a drawer of his three-legged table, which stood at the head of his army cot. He pulled out a roll of vellum. It had been prepared beforehand.

The wily old fox! thought Demetrius. He is always one jump ahead of everyone—friend or foe.

Silva unrolled the parchment and read aloud for the benefit of Demetrius. He spoke in a dramatic voice, like an actor reading his lines in a Greek tragedy.

"Titus, emperor of Rome, *princeps,* first citizen of the Republic, friend and counselor: Silva salutes you and he salutes Rome, center of the universe, beloved son of the gods. Golden city built on the seven hills of Romulus and Remus, we send you greetings!

"Greetings from one who holds the emperor and the empire dear to his heart. And for the emperor and the empire we are ready at all times to give our lives here at Masada.

"Titus, bravest of men, our hearts warm at the encouragement you send us constantly. Without your concern, we here in the desert of Palestine could not hope to succeed. Be assured that we welcome your august advice and experience, and will try to emulate your devotion to the empire and the Republic. Your knowledge of the science of war will be our text to lead us to victory. We long for the day when we may publicly thank you for your assistance. We long for the day when we can return to Rome and the Senate. Be assured that we will hasten our assignment here so that we can return to see the face of our beloved *princeps*.

"With expressions of gratitude and devotion . . ."

When Silva finished reading the letter, he tossed the parchment onto his cot, and his great belly shook at his cleverness.

"It took me an hour to compose yesterday. I can't remember when I had so much fun as I did in dictating this letter to my scribe. It was much more profitable than playing cards with you and the other officers. That isn't amusing, especially when one is losing, as I have done for some time now."

Again his laugh rang out.

Silva picked up the scroll again. He unrolled the parchment and scanned the letter again, relishing every word.

Then he picked up a stylus made of a reed and, with his penknife, sharpened it. Dipping the point into cuttlefish ink, he signed his name with a flourish: "Silva, procurator of Judea."

The slave runner entered at his call. Silva rolled up the parchment and inserted it into a cylindrical case. He handed the case to the runner, saying, "Just in time. *Vale,* good luck. You carry an important message on which a great deal depends. Guard it with your life!"

Silva could scarcely contain his laughter until the runner was out of earshot.

14 / Herod's Palace

The children of Masada adored Urzillah. She understood them. Small and pert, pretty and light-footed like the gazelle from which her name had been taken, she returned their love a thousandfold.

The parents of the children blessed the day that Urzillah had come to them from faraway Nabatea. Though she had come at that black time when Silva had arrived from the north to bring them to their knees, they remembered the girl with gratitude. Thus is it always, they thought. God sends his remedy before the disease. What would they have done with their little ones hanging on to their skirts, crying for attention, grieving at the serious faces and anxious manner of their elders? How much harder it would have been to make preparation for the battle that was so soon to take place!

Urzillah never shirked her duties, but she still managed to find time for her friends, the children. She gave them of her brightness and gaiety. She was just what was needed to make the little ones forget the trials that lay ahead. She made the fort seem less grim by her presence.

There was no one who could make up stories like Urzillah. No one could tell riddles or puzzles the way she did. It took a lot of thinking to find the answers to her riddles. These riddles had been told to her by her father on the long caravan journeys from Petra to the city of Damascus.

What sport there was with Urzillah as the leader! Once again, as they had done before these grim times, the children would skip down the inner staircase that led from the top down through the three levels fashioned by Herod for his palace on the north side of the rock. Luxuriously they would savor the shade and beauty as they held on to the railing that led them below.

At the middle terrace they would stop to play hide-and-seek between the two semicircular walls supporting the uppermost level. How they would laugh at the funny faces she would make to pretend that she was really frightened at their sudden appearance between the columns. And when her turn came to hide, she would slip between the walls as easily as they did.

The real treat lay on the lowest terrace, where the pillars rose to afford them a magnificent frame for the view of the wadi below. The wadi at present was without much water though it was known to fill during the spring, thus providing water for the cisterns below the floor of the rock.

A buttress wall behind them ran from north to east and formed a solid base for the pillars and for the arches between the pillars. The gay party sat down on the benches. Behind them the wall was painted in panels consisting of red and green stripes bordered in black and red on a background veined to resemble real marble.

Urzillah was telling them the enthralling stories

that she had learned from her father. The children listened intently. When she finished there was new sport for them. They observed a Roman guard in the camp far below. He had heard their voices in the clear mountain air, but he could not hope to touch them with either his spear or his arrows. So Urzillah could indulge in the "language of the wise," which consisted of certain gestures.

Standing there in full sight of the guard, she would stretch out her arm and then bring back her fist in a slow gesture. Whereupon the children facing her would turn their faces entirely away from her. They would then break into great peals of laughter. The "language of the wise" was a sign language used by Jews to speak to each other and bewilder the foreigner. For the Jews who knew the Bible, sign language was easy.

Every Jew knew that the outstretched hand meant "Thou shalt remember what the Lord did unto Pharaoh with His outstretched hand. So shall the Lord, thy God, do unto all the people of whom thou art afraid."

As for the averted face, that was a reference to the verses "And I will surely hide My face in that day for the evil which they have wrought."

This language of pantomime had been of some comfort to the Jews who had no way of avenging themselves when the Romans oppressed them in the marketplaces and on the streets. By using this sign language they were able to release some of the pent-up hatred they felt toward their oppressors. The Romans, unable to accuse the Jews of any crime—for they did not know the meaning of these signs and gestures—were left bewildered.

Now it was time for the children to play their second trick on the Roman guard as they stood between the giant columns. First hallooing to make sure that they were being observed, they would then dash away and disappear in the direction of the hidden staircase. Running helter-skelter up the curving stairs, shielded by the huge pillars, they would chase each other up the remaining flight out into the cliff wall and would emerge on the first level.

The trick was to get up the stairs and to the top as quickly as possible. The Roman guard would again hear a halloo and see them standing on the top of the cliff near the wall separating the palace from the remaining buildings. How the children wished they were near enough to see the bewilderment on the guard's face as he saw them appear and disappear at will.

Urzillah could play the grand lady, too. First she would take her cosmetic palette with its soft camelhair brush. On the palette there was the green and blue she needed for her eyes. Looking into the ivory mirror that she took out of her leather case, she would apply this eyeshadow and then accentuate her eyelashes and eyebrows with black. The rouge pot was next, then the scent bottle for a drop of perfume behind her ears.

Using her comb, she would then pile up her black glossy hair, securing it with pins of copper and gold. She would bring her skirt around her, adjusting it to the length of that of a Roman lady of fashion. Two of the children would be appointed to be her train-bearers, and the rest would act as her party. Together they would proceed slowly in a mock parade to the throne room, Herod's conference room. Solemnly they would cross the colored mosaic floor of the long room to the throne at the end, Urzillah bowing to the imaginary crowds that had come to see the "noble lady."

After they had played "court," they would be children again, hopping from one square to the next on the large mosaic in the hall, taking care to jump only on the black squares; then reversing the game, they would jump only on the white areas.

Dust had accumulated on the heavy purple hangings and lay thick on the floors. The Zealots were much too busy to try to clean the buildings, but their beauty was apparent in spite of the dust.

Sometimes the children felt guilty when they enjoyed the beauty of the architecture. The words of Eleazar rang in their ears.

"Remember," he would say, "these buildings were made by a man who believed that luxury and power were the most important things to live by. So he spent his life exploiting others. The lives that were lost in making this structure were not important to Herod. What was important to Herod and his court was power and the material things that power can obtain.

"We of the children of Aaron abhor these outward signs of riches and power. For us it is enough to live a simple life, dedicated to the greater glory of God."

One day Urzillah found time to take them through the baths, which the Romans had built behind the wall on the north side of the Rock. Here in the furnace room, men had toiled like moles underground. Sweating, they had fed the fires in the huge boilers of bronze and brass with wood. The huge kettles had sent up great clouds of steam, which entered the lead pipes hanging from the ceiling and then traveled beneath the floors to warm the rooms of the palace.

Through other lead pipes the water was carried into the *caldarium*, the warm bath. How nice and warm it must have been in the *caldarium* with its doors closed and no windows to bring down the temperature! Even better was the next room, where the floor and walls were heated and the attendant slaves sprinkled water constantly to make the steam for the bathers.

After this, there was the gentle massage with sweet-smelling oils, at the hands of a skillful slave. Finally the bather took a quick dip in the last tub, which was ice cold; and then in a leisurely fashion he would return and put on his clothes.

In the entrance room, which consisted of cubicles for clothes, the children dropped to the floor and picked out the various patterns in the mosaic tiles. There were pink leaves and pomegranates and vines and fig leaves. Though Herod had loved Greek art, he had not dared to use the human figure in any of his art, for fear of offending the Jews and their Law, which forbade the making of images.

It was hard for the children to return to their own cramped quarters in the casemate section, where there was no such beauty. Fathers and mothers were busy; each home was like a little war factory preparing for the defense of the fort. The children dropped onto their beds in the rooms beside the wall, tired from their day. Soon they were sound asleep.

15/ "How Can I Be Strong ...?"

Yeshu stepped out from his casemate apartment, breathed deeply of the early morning air, skirted the apartment where Aviel was still asleep, and climbed on the parapet of the wall. Below him in the wadi, Roman slaves were already toiling, competing with the massive cranes that were lifting immense boulders to make a strong siege wall, which Silva was putting around the entire area. Every inch of the ground around Masada had to be covered by the wall so that there would be no loophole for escape from the mountain. Even the most difficult places were being blocked by a six-foot-high siege wall of stone.

The slaves crawled along the sides of the ravine, carrying their heavy burdens of stones on their backs to the places on the slopes where they would be needed. Just climbing these inclines would have been difficult enough; with the added weight, the task seemed impossible. But this wall was necessary for Roman security. With it, they were confident—providing they could prevent surprise visits by Jewish sappers who might undermine the stockade. The Romans bore in mind the possibility that the Jews of Masada might use the same strategems that the defenders of Jerusalem had used.

Roman soldiers were assigned the duty of hustling the slaves at their work, and they did not spare the *flagrum*. For the slave, it was a choice of deaths —whether the *flagrum* would tear out his life or whether the canyon below would claim him. Many a slave went hurtling to a quick death in the valley below. A bloodcurdling scream would ring out as he lost his footing and tumbled down, landing on the stones below, a horrible pulp of broken bones and torn flesh. Life was cheap, however, and soon another slave would be brought up as replacement to fill the position and complete the assignment.

Koheleth says: "A live dog is better than a dead lion," Yeshu thought. Evidently these men toiling in front of him had accepted a life of shame because they feared death. By choosing slavery, they hoped to prolong their lives, no matter how miserable their condition might be. They had accepted the words of Koheleth in earnest.

Who commits the greater evil? The man who submits to the lash or the one who wields it? Yeshu asked himself. Is man a machine to be tossed aside when he is no longer useful?

The slaves at work on the hill preferred life at any price. They obeyed their master's whip.

The encirclement was proceeding. Twelve towers, each built eighty yards from its neighbor, were set in the siege wall. Walls were also being built around each of the Roman camps. Caution was the watchword of the Roman general.

Perfection! Always perfection! thought Yeshu.

If only this perfection was spent on doing something good for another human being instead of destroying him.

Even in the dark the Roman soldier would be able to find his way to the road and know exactly where the road would lead. For their roads and camps the Romans conformed to a standard plan, which applied whether they were in Gaul or the Galilee. Not only were the camps built to the same design but even the streets that ran through them were uniformly named. For the Roman soldier, everything was reduced to rote, and what was expected of him was blind obedience. Yeshu was reminded of a million puppets led by a single string whose pull was completely obeyed.

Yeshu had been among the builders in Qumran. He recalled with nostalgia quiet sunbaked brick buildings facing a courtyard. They had painted the buildings white. Between the fruit trees and vines and vegetable gardens there had been pleasant nooks where a man could feast his eyes on green and think of the wonders of nature.

When he and his fellow Essenes had sweated in the sun building the commune, they had toiled for those who sought refuge from the harsh and cruel world. He remembered those who came there and also the orphan children whom they had befriended. Yes, Qumran was built with honest toil and love.

The Romans were mighty builders, but they built for another purpose. They built their great towers into the sky, thinking, like the men of Babel, to scale the ramparts of heaven. But their ambitions would bring them to their own destruction.

Yeshu thought of Herod, who had built this fort of Masada and, when he lost Jerusalem to the Jews and their Parthian allies, had fled to the Romans and with their help had returned to take Jerusalem again.

But Herod was like the Romans—he was a prisoner within his own walls. Only the man of spirit was truly free because his thoughts could range at will.

Vanity of vanities, all is vanity, thought Yeshu. Outside were thousands of soldiers and slaves building so that they could destroy life. He shut his eyes. It had been foretold by the prophets that a great battle would take place between the forces of light and darkness. Well, there it was! It was only a question of time before the great battle would be fought. In that day when the great test came, the Messiah would arise to bring peace to all the people of the world.

Yeshu longed for that day with all his soul.

Only time could tell. But inevitably, he realized, first must come the great confrontation between the tiny nation of Israel and the immense power of Rome.

With a heavy sigh, Yeshu climbed down and returned to his apartment. At the door he met Adin, who was seeking him. A cloud of concern oppressed Adin's usually serene countenance. Adin came to the point immediately. What he had to tell had depressed him and sapped his will. He needed somebody to turn to with his problem, but everybody at Masada had his own private sorrow to bear. Then he had thought of Yeshu. He was wise, he had seen life, and he knew Ohada, having traveled with them through the desert.

"Yeshu, I have come to you for advice. Only you can help me."

Ohada had been having nightmares—night after night, always the same dream.

"You know Ohada," Adin said, "how strong she is and determined, but she seems to have cracked under the strain. With the coming of the baby, she has become entirely different. Suddenly she has started to worry. In the desert, when all we had was a skin bag of water and a crust of bread, you know how wonderfully brave she was. I remember one night before we joined you, we had to hide because a band of robbers had camped near the road. We hid in the rocks all night, but she was beautifully calm.

"But now she is full of fear. She sees her grandmother holding out her hands and insisting that she must take the baby away to save him from danger. Ohada wakes up in a sweat. She is convinced that she will lose Yehudah—that Yehudah is about to die.

"At the same time she has made me swear that I will kill the baby rather than let him be taken away from us. There is nothing I can say that will assure her that we will always be together."

To Yeshu's mind suddenly there came the hymn of the Essenes:

"I am the product of clay and fashioned from water.
How can I be wise unless Thou hast created me?
How can I talk unless Thou hast opened my mouth?
How can I answer unless Thou hast made me wise?
How can I be strong unless Thou hast established me?"

Into Yeshu's face there came the expression of a shepherd bending over one of his flock that has been hurt by a wild animal. Thus might Moses have looked when he saw how the Egyptians tormented the Jews. He remembered his own hurt when he arrived at

Qumran searching for the truth. How does a person who has lost his wife and children give comfort to a young man in distress? Yeshu recalled the day he returned from a journey to his house in Sepphoris, to find that he was alone. His wife and daughters had left him, unable to bear the poverty any longer.

It seemed to him incongruous for one with his tragedies to advise a man in Adin's situation. Adin was not the only one in camp whose nerves had been reaching the breaking point; what comfort could he offer the young man?

The lines of the hymn recurred to him: "How can I be strong unless Thou hast established me?"

So he let Adin speak until his story was told and the burden released from his mind. Adin would not have come unless he was desperate.

"This is your first child, Adin," Yeshu said. "You will find out in time that women sometimes become very anxious about their babies. Then, too, Ohada has been under stress for a long time, though she has successfully hidden her nervousness. Try once again to tell her how much you love her; tell her that you have come through the hardest part together and that her grandmother has come to her in her dream to show her love for the child. The spirits of your ancestors cherish you; they are part of every family. We are bound up with the people who came before us in ties that cannot be dissolved. Tell her that the child—all of you—are not alone.

"I will come and speak to her in a few minutes. Give me time to make up a potion of herbs to calm her and give her peaceful sleep. It is best so."

When Adin left, Yeshu for the first time in years

allowed himself to dwell on the family he had lost through no fault of his own. He remembered that his wife had come to him with pathetic tales about the nightmares she had been having and begged for help. He had not understood at the time how troubled women can become when tensions build up in them.

As he remembered, sobs shook the frame of the gentle Essene. Then he dried his tears and went to help Ohada and Adin.

16 / The Gods Have Spoken!

The watchers above gazed down at the Romans with fascinated repulsion. A Jew needed a strong stomach to observe the pagan rites unfolding before him. Urzillah was sickened. Brave and unafraid though she was, she could not bear the blasphemy and the barbarity.

Beneath the walls of Masada and in plain sight of all, a ceremony was being performed which Roman armies observed before going into battle. The first act had already been played with Calvus the *haruspex,* the soothsayer, as chief actor. The old man had sat on his throne in the broad main street of the Roman camp in front of the chief officers' quarters. His eyes were shrewd and his long fingers fluttered in the air above him, always tracing squares, large and small. He muttered in a strange gibberish that was neither Greek nor Latin. It was the ancient tongue of the Romans—the Etruscan language—and since it was not understood by the soldiers about him, it sounded like a magical incantation. The gods were speaking to their earthly representatives in a language that only they could understand. By means of divination, called the *auspicium,* the gods would send their messages and advice through old Calvus.

All had been silent as the old man watched the

skies, constantly muttering and forming his squares in the air. When the proper bird appeared in the special square that he indicated in the sky above him, the *haruspex* would decide whether or not the signs were favorable for the army to attack the walls before them.

No one would ever know which birds were considered auspicious. That was the secret locked in the mysteries of the men who served as *augurs*, divines. They would hand on their knowledge to their sons, thus keeping the profession in their families and their privileges from generation to generation.

The waiting had seemed endless, but no one dared to speak to the seer or interrupt him. With the setting sun, a silent anticipation seized the crowd. A giant eagle of the desert appeared, flying over the camp twice in leisurely fashion, forming each time an almost perfect square above the mountain fortress. The seer stood up from his chair, his head raised to the heavens, his right hand on his crooked staff, and his left hand extended to the bird. He muttered phrases which seemed jubilant and triumphant. The gods had spoken. The sign had come. The commander could now be assured of success.

The silence gave way to a shout.

A pig was led to the altar. Its head was decorated with flowers and its snout and ears were gilded. Several half-naked men of the priestly class held the animal. Silva had now taken his place at the altar. He stood waiting for the animal to be brought up to him. Then he placed his hands upon the gilded head and stepped aside for the priest who stood near him. Calvus, who had changed into an embroidered toga and wore a pointed cap tipped with olive wood on his head, advanced, bearing in his hand the crooked staff that was taller than himself.

With his left hand he threw a fold of the toga over his head and then began to intone a prayer for the sacrifice. The participants stood reverently, their thoughts supposedly fixed on divine matters. The attendants who held the animals, upon a sign from the priest, cut a few hairs from between the pig's eyes and threw them into the fire. Then two attendants brought down their axes at the same time on the animal's head so that it was knocked unconscious. A third stabbed the animal and caught the cascading blood in a silver basin. Another slash and the animal's entrails streamed out from a gaping hole.

The *haruspex* reached in for the liver, withdrew it, and seemed to be examining it very carefully. The altar by this time was awash with blood, as were the priests and the attendants around it. Finally, in one dramatic gesture, the high priest raised the liver for all to see as he spoke in a firm voice.

"Bene," he said. *"Est bene.* It is good."

The omen was favorable.

The soldiers stood by, pleased, and convinced that victory would be theirs. The blood-spattered proceedings seemed to them very suitable as a preliminary to battle. They had long been accustomed to such sights.

The ceremony continued. A young boy offered a basin of gold filled with water to the priest, who, with great deliberation, washed his hands and then dried them on a small towel of purest white. A young lamb was led to the altar. The music continued. While the lamb waited, the first offering was sprinkled with

meal, wine, and incense. A giant fire by this time had been built nearby. The pig was burnt, and then attention was fastened on the lamb.

Urzillah could stand the sight no longer and fled from the scene. The girl took the children who were gathered around her to the steps of the south cistern where they would be free from the sights and sounds of the idolatrous ceremony below.

"But do we not also have sacrifices?" one of the children asked her.

Iddo spoke; he had seen the Temple sacrifices when he was quite small, and his priestly family had participated in their performance.

"According to Jewish Law, the slaughter must be done in a very humane manner and must be performed at a good distance from the altar and very quietly. We are told in our Torah: 'The blood is the life,' so that the animals are slaughtered as quickly as possible and with the least pain."

This explanation seemed to satisfy the children.

Below, the ceremony continued. After the sacrifice of the lamb, the priest stood upright, his hands raised to the skies. Several assistants then sprang into action. They danced and leaped about the altar, chanting incantations in the ancient language of the priests. Victory would be with Rome. Jove would prove mightier than Jehovah.

17/ Is There Hope?

Silva's road lay like a huge sword, its blade turned threateningly toward Masada and its defenders. Indeed, by the light of the moon, the white limestone quarried from the neighborhood with which the road was paved had a luminous quality that was ghostly. It gave the watchers above an eerie feeling of impending doom. Try as they might, they could not shake this mood.

The lower part of the road was quite narrow, but after a distance of three hundred feet it led to a great bank of large stones, which formed a platform about one hundred feet wide and strong enough to hold the biggest and heaviest of the war machines without collapsing.

Roman engineers prided themselves on their efficiency, and with good reason. The base of the platform consisted of the cedars that were the pride of the Lebanese forests, which had been cut and transported to this spot by slave labor from Syria. Upon these trunks were laid great rocks taken from the canyon below, raised by Roman cranes and by the men. Last, there was the limestone brought up from the side of the cliff on the backs of slaves or in the baskets of the soldiers. The base stood at a height of almost four hundred feet, so all hands were needed to keep the work moving relentlessly forward.

It had taken two weeks to build the road and the ledge on the west side. Silva had decided to attack from the west after taking a trip around Masada with his engineers and haughtily inspecting the four sides. Actually, the platform was possible only from this side; the other sides had no point at which a platform could have been built. Upon announcing his decision, Silva had given his engineers but two weeks to finish their gigantic construction.

Eleazar ben Ya'ir was relieved to know once and for all where the attack would be launched. Though the Zealots had already prepared some stones for ammunition at other places, ben Ya'ir now concentrated his energies on putting his war supplies on the west side. A constant guard was still kept on the other sides, together with some supplies, but it was clear what tactics Silva had decided upon.

The pile of rocks on the west side where the path came up grew from day to day, in preparation for the time when the action would begin. To this pile the Zealots added sections of the great pillars they had taken earlier from the summer palace on the north side. For many days, the Zealots had been dismantling the pillars and rolling them to the places where they would be needed. Herod's pride would have suffered had he seen how his architectural triumph was reduced to a rock pile.

At night, under cover of darkness, the Zealots, who knew every inch of the mountain, would climb down to the platform still under construction and attempt to disrupt the work by tearing gaps among the stones, smearing pitch on the logs, and setting them afire. Often the day's work was ruined.

Silva stationed guards there at night to keep watch. The Zealots' attempts at sabotage became too dangerous and too costly. Finally, they stopped.

When the Roman troops and engineers came close enough to the wall, the Zealots' stores of stones were put to use. The missiles took their toll of Silva's men.

"The platform must be built," he said to the officer who came to complain to Silva of the heavy losses suffered at the hands of the Jews.

"A gift to Rome," Nathaniel said grimly as he rolled down a particularly beautiful section of a Herodian pillar. The stones, weighing over two hundred pounds and coming over the edge of the wall at tremendous speed, took a gang of road-builders by surprise, and many were crushed under its weight.

Adin watched in silence. Strange, he thought, these stones were meant to represent Herod's pride and power. Now, used as a weapon in the name of God, they have become an instrument to fight oppression and oppressors, cursed be they.

To counter this form of attack, the Romans used the tortoise formation, the *testudo*. Fitting their shields closely together above their heads and by their sides, the soldiers provided a cover for the construction work. Thus most of the stones were deflected and scarcely an arrow found its way to the workers. This tactic of forming a huge human screen tied up many soldiers, but the work of building the platform proceeded safely and quickly.

Eleazar now called for the next step in his tactics

for the defense of the fort. There was nothing else now but to use the pitch and asphalt they had brought up from the Dead Sea. They heated it over great fires and poured it down on the tortoise formations. Using great ladles and buckets, the Zealots stood in the recesses of the walls or on the turrets and spilled those scalding substances on the troops.

The screams of the Roman soldiers as the burning pitch stuck to their armor and began to sear them was ear-splitting. Shrieking in agony, some of the soldiers lost their balance on the hillside and went hurtling down the canyon to the stones below.

Eleazar was everywhere, making sure that the Zealots pressed hard against the attacking Romans. He encouraged his men to deeds of bravery, himself taking a leading part by standing on the turrets and picking out the Roman officers for his personal attention.

The ramp cost the Romans many lives, but when the towers were finally mounted on the platform, the real onslaught would begin. The Romans knew this, and the Zealots knew it full well, too.

At last the platform was completed, and Silva was able to order that the towers be brought out. These movable towers of wood were about sixty feet tall. They came up the incline, trundled on wheels like lumbering elephants while the soldiers pushed, under the direction of their officers. Finally, in spite of the defenders' efforts they arrived in position.

On the lower shelves of the towers, great slings of logs tipped with iron and bronze hung loose in their cradles. Their purpose was to pound against the wall with great force, so as to breach it. On the upper levels, soldiers in the tortoise formation protected the soldiers manning the slings.

Other weapons of assault were great catapults capable of throwing huge stones into the fort behind the walls, crushing anybody who happened to be in the way. These white stones had been hewn from the cliff. Because of their color, they could quite easily be seen against the sun.

"The stone is coming!" would be the cry of the Zealots. Since its flight was slow, those in its path were often able to save themselves. To increase the effectiveness of the bombardment, the Romans changed the color of the stones to render them less visible.

All elements of the Roman attack now came into operation—the ram against the wall, the arrows pouring into the fort, and the stones catapulted over the walls. The Jews' defense consisted of the bowmen who stood on the walls and turrets, picking off the men at the machines, the huge stones that were sent hurtling down to crush the machines of war, and occasionally the pitch and asphalt in the great kettles.

Eventually the greater strength of the Romans began to have its effect. Their machines breached the walls. A great shout rose from the Roman army. They saw success about to crown their armed efforts.

But Eleazar had prepared for this contingency. Leaving a skeleton force on the walls, he had brought out all the Zealots, men, women, and children, and set them to work placing great timbers from Herod's palace in a new barrier on the inside of the opening in the Herodian wall. Having raised these logs into position, they filled the spaces between with sand, soil,

and stones. With spade and basket, they toiled all
through the night. By morning they had built an
earthen wall that was held up by the great timbers.

In the morning Silva was bewildered. His plans
had called for a complete breach of the walls on that
day in the month of Nissan. Now, to find out just what
had happened, he himself mounted a siege tower for
a closer look. He was furious when he realized that
instead of breaking the wall apart, every blow of his
battering ram was now packing the earth of the inner

tower wall into an unbreakable rampart. With every jolt of the vicious ram, the earth became firmer and more compact inside its scaffolding. A wall was being forged that would be impossible to breach. So Silva wisely called off the rams, and the Jews gained relief from the incessant pounding. It seemed as though the mighty power of the Romans had been brought to a halt. God was good. He was with His people.

But Eleazar did not share the elation of the others. He knew that the next phase would follow immediately. Rome knows no failures, he thought. They would find a way. When the next step was taken, Jewish ingenuity would have to begin to work again.

Though he was not lulled into any sense of false security, Eleazar praised his men and suggested a communal celebration when Passover came. He fixed the fifteenth of Nissan as the date. Perhaps the miracle of Pesach would be enacted again in their own time. Perhaps once again the people of Israel would be delivered from tyranny.

Adin heard the words of Eleazar. He ran off, tired though he was, to tell Iddo and the other children about the celebration of the festival.

His messages heartened the children. Sleep was better that night as they dreamed of the Seder table and of its warmth and joy.

Sarah, Justus's wife, was especially happy. Passover was the holiday that appealed most to her. It was the first religious festival she had celebrated with her husband's family after her conversion. She immediately set out for the ritual bath and was the first to arrive at the mikveh on the south wall.

The bathhouse was not like the luxurious Roman

bath. It was a simple system, consisting of a small pool for washing hands and feet, then a larger bath for immersion. As required by religious law, this latter pool was filled partly with rainwater drawn from a rainwater cistern adjacent to it. Sarah and the other women of the community performed their ablutions, and as she did this, she savored the festival to come.

18 / Is There One God?

"Where is this God of the Jews? Where does He keep Himself? How can we hope to conquer something we cannot touch or see? What is His power? Who is He? Why can this God of the Jews look down on us while we cannot find him? How long can He mock us?"

Silva paced up and down. The frantic tone of his voice showed that he was disturbed. His whole way of life and his beliefs were being challenged. Being a Roman, he had been taught that to propitiate the gods insured success. Yet, though he had performed the proper rites and brought the offerings required of him, he was losing the battle. It shook his belief in the Roman way of life, in which he had been raised and which he had never questioned. Success had always been his in the past. For the first time he was unnerved and bewildered by a situation that was contrary to his experience. He was afraid.

Silva was a practical man. He had carefully followed the rules of warfare. Success had been within his grasp. There had been months of careful planning and preparation, backbreaking work on which he had staked his future. He had refused to be hurried into making any moves before he was ready. He had supervised every phase of the operations himself. Now, when the enemy was hopelessly caged in before him and victory had seemed certain, the whim of the wind (or was it the God of the Jews?) had turned all to failure.

Silva continued pacing up and down, muttering.

"Vespasian thought of himself as a god. Nero, too, would have us believe that he was a god, though we laughed at his pot belly. But both of them were visible and, like the *lares* and *penates* of our household, could be touched. By Jupiter, all peoples have visible gods—except the Jews. This Elohim they call upon is intangible. Nobody can put a finger on Him, they claim. He comes and goes with the wind.

"I've asked these Jews, 'Where can your God be found?'

" 'Everywhere!' they answer.

" 'If He is everywhere,' I ask, 'why can I not see Him?'

" 'We know He is there, because He reveals Himself by signs,' they say.

"Well," said Silva, and he shook his fist in emphasis, "this wind we depended on must be one of His signs. His sign. With the wind He protects the Jews against the mighty Roman army and our gods.

"With such a God these Jews need no arms. We threw torches into their camp. . . ."

Silva was becoming more and more agitated. Demetrius was sorely afraid that he would do something rash to himself. The aide-de-camp thanked the gods that he was not the commander in chief. Authority and rank carried too many responsibilities. Success or failure was always attributed to the leader.

"We threw torches into their camp to burn the timbers of the wall they built. We counted on the wind, which generally blows to the south every evening at this time. The torches were soaked with petroleum and bitumen from the Asphalt Sea. We planned every part of our strategy—yet, by Hercules, a God we cannot see, that no one can see, has outwitted us by blowing the fire back into our faces."

As Silva spoke, Demetrius heard the noise of the soldiers in the camp, shouting for water and sand to put out the fire, which had caught the canvas of the tents and the leather of their baggage stacked outside. Sparks were flying furiously around them, carried from one part of the camp to the other by sudden gusts of wind. Demetrius wondered how long it would take for the flames to reach them, but Silva seemed unconscious of the danger. With an effort Demetrius listened to what Silva was saying.

"Tell me, Demetrius, is it possible for this invisible Being to overcome a power as mighty as Rome? Can He really defeat Titus? Ridiculous. Yet I tell you, Demetrius, if all our work is to be destroyed in one moment, as it seems now, I am ready to add the invisible God to my gods. I would even join the Israelites, since the stronger god must prevail."

Demetrius wondered idly how one could possibly worship a God that was invisible. He imagined a niche among the household *lares* and *penates,* a niche elaborately decorated but empty because the Jewish God was invisible. He wiped the smile off his face, but Silva was not looking at him. He was much too occupied to notice anything around him.

"There are those who are joining the Jews," he said. "In Rome a friend told me about one of his servants who had become a New Israelite. The servant talked about his new religion, which tells of the coming of a Jewish king who will overcome the power of Rome. It sounded so fantastically foolish at the time, and I laughed it off as being impossible."

"Yet," Demetrius spoke as he continued listening for the roar of the flames, "I hear that most Jews do not accept this idea. They follow the men whom they call the prophets, who predicted there will be a time when all men will put down their arms and never again wage war."

Demetrius, too, seemed to have some knowledge of the beliefs of the Jews.

"One does not know what to believe," Silva answered. "The New Israelites, who are also called Christians, say this king has already come and that he was crucified in the time of our procurator Pontius Pilate. They believe that he will come again to bring peace to the world. These Jews do not agree, even among themselves. But I tell you, Demetrius, we must not underestimate the Jewish God."

Just then a shout arose from the men in the camp. Silva and Demetrius only had time to reach the opening of the tent when one of the centurions came to them on the run. He pointed exultantly toward the Jewish fort, and they could see from where they stood that the summit of the hill was streaked with fire, for the wind had changed and was now blowing toward the fort.

"The fire—the gods are with us, the oracle spoke truly," the centurion was stuttering. The words spilled from his mouth.

Silva took the situation in at a glance. The logs in the earthen wall of the fort were beginning to flare up.

"Post a strong guard. See to it that not one of the enemy escapes. We will pick up our singed doves in the morning. Let them warm themselves by the fire of our torches. Perhaps their God will burn with them, even though He cannot be seen."

The old Silva had returned.

19 / Free At Last

Ohada and Adin often discussed Eleazar during those days of the siege, as they used to do while they were still in Babylonia. Now, as then, he was still their idol, a heroic figure who had transformed their lives and the pattern of their existence. He was, all acknowledged, a true leader, totally dedicated to the cause and well able to convey his ideals to the men and women who worked with him, fought with him, and dreamed of freedom.

To Ohada and Adin, he seemed a personality from the Bible. They compared him to Joshua.

Adin and Ohada were often puzzled about Eleazar. Though Eleazar lived with all of them in close proximity, he still seemed alone. Tonight, oppressed by foreboding and fearful of their future, they understood why. A commander stood alone, separated by his responsibility from all others. The life of the community was in his hands; the burden of this knowledge was always with him. Perhaps this was why he had never remarried when his wife had died on the way to Masada.

Now he was standing in the place he usually occupied at the altar of the synagogue. The community of Masada was assembled about him on the stone benches of the converted Roman amphitheater.

Behind them, the flames of the burning wall rumbled and lit the area. Ohada could see quite plainly the contented face of Yehudah, who was asleep in her arms.

Eleazar spoke directly to their hearts and as always seemed to be echoing their thoughts. His words were filled with sadness.

"God has deserted us," he began heavily. "Providence has decreed our destruction. Wind and fire have combined to destroy our wall and our hope of victory. We believed we were the instrument of God, by whom the Romans would have been driven from our land and Jewish freedom restored. Unfortunately, this was not to be our destiny."

He paused for a long moment, then continued.

"The strength of our fortress and of our determination was not sufficient to bring us success. Success depends upon who is higher than ourselves, not merely upon our arms or the walls of Masada.

"Tonight God spoke to us through the wind. In His voice we were able to hear very plainly that we had failed. These things have not come to pass because of the power of the Romans. Nor did they come to pass because we were weak. These happenings are God's sign to show us that we have sinned. We are not worthy. This has been decided by a wisdom greater than ours. This we must accept."

Weeping could be heard in the congregation—weeping and the tearing of garments in grief. It was not only the old women who were crying. Men, too, hardened warriors, felt streams of tears course down their cheeks.

Filled with grief, Ohada and Adin looked at each

other and at the innocent face of their sleeping child. Seeking at least some hope, Ohada's eyes sought out the young warriors. Perhaps they would offer a way out. The faces of Baruch and Nachum were grim and stony. They sat unmoving, staring at Eleazar, waiting for the word of their commander.

Faithful to the death, they were resigned to the will of Eleazar. They, like the rest of the community, were waiting for their commander to decide how the end should come. Ohada's eyes turned back to the altar.

Eleazar did not delay his decision; he spoke with quiet compassion. "We have to decide what course of action we are to take. In the morning, the army of Silva will come through the gap in the wall. We could continue fighting; we could bar the way with our bodies, as we did in Jerusalem. But how long would we be able to stand up against the strength of Silva's army? All we could do would be to show our determination to the last. But there is a greater consideration we must think of: our wives and children.

"What will become of them when we are gone?"

The weeping of the women grew louder; the men no longer sat immobile; their horror was etched in their faces.

Men and women held each other in desperation. Aviel saw his father bow his head and break out into sobs as he held his mother tightly. Until that day Aviel had never seen tears on his father's face.

"There is only one thing we can do to save them."

Eleazar spoke with great resolution. "Men would be put to the rack, and tortured with fire and flogging. Those who were left alive would be preserved to make sport and laughter for the conquerors.

"But the fate of the men would be as nothing compared to the fate of the women and children.

"All men must die in due time. It is so written. The coward and the brave have the same end.

"But not to leave our wives and children in the hands of Romans—that is a decision we can make by ourselves."

Though the word suicide was not used, each one understood what had to be done. The community hardened its mind on a common resolution.

Now they had only to decide how it would be done.

Eleazar guided them in his calm manner. He pulled from behind him, near the Torah ark, a vase into which he proceeded to put ten shards. On each shard he had written the names of nine of his officers and his own. The name of Nathaniel, his second-in-command was there, as was that of Justus, the Alexandrian. These were the men who would complete what the others could not.

"My brothers and sisters," Eleazar continued, "this is what we must do. You will wish to spend what time still remains with your loved ones and say farewell before we prepare ourselves. In the hour before the sun rises for the morning prayers, we will assemble here. We will also destroy the stores so that Silva will not profit from them or from the Temple offerings and the gold we have saved."

Yeshu spoke up. "Our Torah scrolls must be made safe from contamination."

Nathaniel added, "Let us show these heathen that we could have held out for some time with our supplies. Let us leave just one warehouse untouched."

"It is a good thought," said Eleazar. "Let us also

destroy our personal possessions and our chambers and wreak as much destruction as we can."

Huldah and Urzillah sat together, listening to the plans being made. With them sat some of the children of the community, including Iddo. They had become closely attatched to each other and now clung together for comfort.

Eleazar left them all with the words of assurance they needed.

"While freedom is our own, and while we are in possession of our swords, let us preserve our liberties. Let us die free men gloriously surrounded by our wives and children. Let us snatch the prize from the hands of the enemy and leave them nothing but our dead bodies."

The Zealots rose as one man to prepare for their next meeting, which would be their last. Each family returned to its home to prepare for the end.

Huldah and Urzillah, however, made their way to the south cistern, and the children went with them for the solace they so much needed in their nervous state.

The sound of flames could be heard around them as they walked.

Inside the cistern, the children fell into a troubled sleep. The old woman and the young Nabatean talked together in whispers.

20 / "Death to the Jews!"

Silva scarcely closed his eyes that night. He roamed the camp to make sure that the guards were alert to foil anyone who might try to escape from the fort above. That no one tried did not surprise him in the least. He had seen the courage of the Jews and their fearless acceptance of death.

However, one could never know what new tactics these Jews would improvise. Silva did not dare take anything for granted. So preparations for the final taking of Masada were planned with the usual care.

The air was cool and pleasant on this spring morning of the fifteenth of Nissan. The sun seemed to smile on the activities of the Romans. The birds flitted in and out among the rocks, hunting for insects.

Huge siege towers with their great armored arches were again wheeled into position by the engineers. Once again the rams began their work against the fire-blackened walls, which now crumbled as the great timbers pounded against them. The din made it a scene of pandemonium, in the middle of which were the Roman soldiers bent under the tortoise, waiting for the usual shower of missiles and arrows. But nothing came.

Nevertheless many a Roman soldier standing to

arms for the assault could be seen secretly touching the charm at his throat to make sure that his luck would hold out. Huge sections of wall gave way. The vibrations of the rams were succeeded by the sound of drum and trumpet. Silva was signaling that the openings were now wide enough for the cohorts to force their way through. The assault was on.

They came up the ramp six abreast.

"Death to the Jews! Death to the Jews!"

A jubilant spirit seemed to seize the Roman soldiers as they moved forward. Though the end had not yet come, it now seemed inevitable—after three years. Before them lay the final action. There would be plenty of goods for all to take after they had killed the Jews. Perhaps there would be money, too.

While the bowmen kept watch, the infantry began to swarm through the breaches. Then the men who had manned the huge siege towers entered the fort from the top of their high edifices, dropping in from above. The Romans entered Masada in huge waves.

The inside of the fort was not unfamiliar to the Romans. From the siege towers they had been able to look over the wall and examine the arrangements. Every time they had hurled their great stones from the towers, they had peered into the area below.

But they were not prepared for the scene now spread before them. The corpses of nearly a thousand people lay fallen in little family groups. The distance between each group was only a few feet. It was as though the comrades sought to lend each other support even in death.

They had met death without a struggle and each

lay as though asleep. Only the streams of blood flowing from their wounds testified to the fact that they were indeed dead. The little children lay in the arms of their mothers, and the mothers lay in the arms of their husbands. The families had not been separated by defeat.

The Romans exclaimed to each other at the sight, even while they fanned out to find the living. Silva, following hard on the heels of his infantry, was shocked into silence. As he looked, he felt reluctant admiration for these people who would not yield even in death. He had heard how the inhabitants of Jerusalem had bared their necks to the knives of the Roman procurator, begging to be killed rather than to have to bow down to the statue of the emperor Gaius Caligula in the Temple. Now he saw what freedom and their rebellion meant to them. They preferred death to losing either. Such devotion Silva could not understand; but he could admire it.

"Find me Eleazar ben Ya'ir," he ordered his *legatus*. This officer beckoned to a Jewish slave taken at the fall of Jerusalem, who had known the Jewish leader and could testify to the identity of the commander of Masada.

Eleazar was not hard to find. He lay at the head of the little army near a jar of red clay. Ten shards were scattered beside the jar and on each shard was the name of a subordinate commander of the fort, including that of Nathaniel. It was plain to see that they had drawn lots after each leader had taken care of his own family and seen to his relatives and friends. Then Eleazar ben Ya'ir, who had drawn the final task, had killed his comrades and fallen on his own weapon.

Death had cheated the Romans of their revenge. For years they had been powerless against a small group of defenders who had held them at bay. Now the Romans stood helpless in the midst of the dead.

"This is a peculiar people," said Silva to Demetrius.

"Peculiar indeed!" said Demetrius.

"Let us see whether we may still find someone alive," said Silva. "Let the men spread out through the camp and search well. Do not forget that there are underground cisterns and perhaps tunnels."

Everywhere, however, there were smoldering ruins. Great beams had fallen from the high ceilings of the palace onto the mosaic floor below. In the casemate rooms against the walls, fires built by each family had consumed their private possessions. The sacredness of the Jewish family had been preserved from desecration by the pagan invader.

In some of the rooms, cooking pots stood with the evening meal, which the family had not eaten and now would never eat. This was to have been their Passover Seder.

The work of destruction had been hurried but it had been quite thorough. The storerooms had been gutted and the oil and wine of the great jars mingled with the olives and wheat and salt to make a great congealed mass on the floor. Only one storeroom had been left intact, with its contents.

Silva was a discerning man and he could understand the significance of this gesture.

"This has been done to show their contempt for

us. By this, they have demonstrated two things. First, they show us that in spite of all our efforts to blockade them, they had enough to eat. Second, they wanted to make sure that we would not profit from their stores."

"Jerusalem did not have this wealth of good food," Demetrius reminded him.

"No," Silva agreed. "It was not because of starvation that these Zealots killed themselves. It was because of their hatred for us. To them we were savages. And they were certain that they were the people chosen by God."

Also untouched was one large alabaster vessel containing pure olive oil. The jar was marked with a strange inscription in Hebrew. Silva stopped in front of this jar and called on the Jewish slave to give them an explanation.

"These are the offerings to the Temple, which the Zealots had been saving for the time when the Temple was again to be in Jewish hands. It was their hope to serve their God in the Temple and to sacrifice to Him again in Jerusalem."

"Strange again," said Silva. "They must have hoped to the very last minute. Their hopes died only with the wind last night."

There were few spoils for the Romans. The storerooms were disappointing, and there was no gold or silver to be found anywhere. A large number of copper coins were scattered around. They were of Jewish coinage; some bore the words YEAR ONE OF THE FREEDOM OF ZION, others YEAR TWO OF THE FREEDOM OF ZION, and there were still others coined in the third year of the revolt. They had never been used.

The soldiers refused to pick up the copper coins. It wasn't worth the effort.

"Strange," said Silva again. "Strange that we see none of those scrolls for which they have always been willing to give up their lives."

"Perhaps they have been burned," suggested Demetrius. "That is just as well, since our soldiers are fearful of the witchcraft written on the sheepskins. However, I see why the Jews took such an action. I remember that some of our soldiers are in the habit of defacing or contaminating the scrolls of the Jews to show their contempt for the Jewish religion."

A shout from a group of soldiers who had been searching for booty with very little success sent Silva's staff hurrying to the entrance of one of the cisterns. Silva hoped that they had taken some prisoners; he wanted to speak with those he had conquered. There were many questions he wanted to ask of them.

It was too late. The prisoners lay dead on the steps of a large cistern in the center of the area. There was a young girl and a boy of about twelve years. In the hands of the boy was a knife of the kind that the Sicarii carried.

The soldier who stood nearest the three was angry.

"The boy attacked me. I was only trying to be friendly with the girl. We had to kill them both when she tried to help him."

Silva was about to turn away when his eyes lighted with expectation. An old woman stumbled up the steps, prodded on by a soldier. She was brought before Silva for questioning. She identified herself by the name of Huldah, the aunt of Eleazar ben Ya'ir.

She described how the people had sacrificed themselves. She said that the girl, whom she called Urzillah, had taken some children when the situation seemed hopeless and had comforted them on the steps of the cistern where she was accustomed to take them to tell them stories.

Silva turned to the soldier, hoping for some further information that would be useful.

"Did the girl say anything?" asked Silva. He could imagine how the rough soldier had tried to be "friendly" to this gentle girl. She was dressed in a fine robe of silk. It had been torn in her struggle with the man.

"The boy shouted, 'I'll not let him touch you, Urzillah; I'll kill the Roman swine.' What could I do but kill them?" the legionary asked.

"Let them lie there. Living, they might have been of use. Dead, they are carrion."

Silva turned away.

Then, speaking to Demetrius, he said, "Have all the bodies thrown over the edge of the ravine. The jackals and vultures will feast tonight. We will occupy the fort of Masada as a sign that we have proven the might of Rome."

"What shall we do with the woman?"

"She cannot be of any use to us or to anyone. Get rid of her."

There was only one more group to be found. They lay near the cold pool of the Roman bathhouse. It was a small family, consisting of a young father, a pretty mother, and a baby. Their bodies were still warm, as though they had clung to life together for as long as they dared. A sandal of the young woman lay nearby.

It was the sandal she had worn on the road between Babylonia and Masada.

"It is finished," said Flavius Silva.

And he turned away.

Epilogue

The scrolls for which the Romans searched were finally found in the year 1964. Gentle hands unearthed the jars in which the scrolls had been hidden under the synagogue floor. The dry soil of the desert had preserved them.

There were the Books of Deuteronomy, Ezekiel, and Leviticus, and there were a few chapters from the Book of Psalms. They were identical to the Bible of today. Yeshu's scroll of the Book of Jubilees that had entertained Ohada on her trek from Qumran was in good condition, as was the Sabbath Sacrifices of the Essenes.

There was also the book called the Wisdom of Ben-Sira, or Ecclesiasticus, which Yeshu had read to Aviel. To scholars this find was important, since it proved for the first time that Ben-Sira had written his original work in the language of his people—Hebrew.

Urzillah and Iddo lay on the cistern steps where they had been killed, as did Huldah, who seems to have shared their fate after all. Perhaps the soldier could not be bothered dragging them to the wall and throwing them over. He also overlooked the pretty mirror, which had fallen into the rubble.

The little family of Adin was left where they had fallen, to be discovered twenty centuries later.

Hundreds of silver coins were found buried under the floors. The Roman soldiers had been denied their spoils.

When Silva said, "It is finished," he had not reckoned with the destiny of the Jewish people.

Today thousands upon thousands of people visit Masada every year to pay tribute to a brave band of men and women who fought for freedom in their lifetime and who fell on their swords rather than be taken alive by the Romans.

The modern Israeli soldier, remembering the tragedy of Masada, takes this vow when he is sworn into his army:

"*Shainit Metzada Lo Teepol!* Masada will not fall again!"

Words Used
at the Time of the Zealots

ABAYA   A cloak covering for desert-dwellers.

AUGUR   A priest who officiated at Roman religious
         ceremonies, predicting and advising.

AUSPICIUM   The decision of the Roman gods as in-
             terpreted by *augurs*.

BAR or BEN   Son of.

CALDARIUM   A room for a hot bath.

CASEMATE   A room built between the two walls of a
            fort.

CIRCUMVALLATION   A wall built around a besieged
                   fort to prevent escape and to
                   protect the attacking army.

CISTERN   A reservoir to hold water.

CUIRASS   A part of the armor made to protect the
           body, made up of a breastplate and back-
           plate fastened together.

DECAPOLIS   Ten cities built by Rome to guard the Palestine frontier.

EDOM   The country stretching from the Dead Sea to the Red Sea and from the Arabian desert to Eilat in the west.

EDOMITES   The people of Edom. They were independent until conquered by Hyrcanus, one of the strongest of the Maccabean kings, who then converted the Edomites to Judaism.

ESSENES   During the first century B.C.E., a group of Jews separated themselves from the Pharisee movement and settled near the Dead Sea. There they lived a communal life and purified themselves symbolically by immersion in water.

GREAVES   Armor for the legs below the knees.

GULLI GULLI   Like our modern *hocus pocus* or *abracadabra*.

HARUSPEX   Like the *augur*. The *haruspex* foretold the future by examining the liver, heart, and so on of animals killed in sacrifice.

KEFEYA   A head covering made of linen or cotton, worn by desert-dwellers to protect the neck as well as the head.

KHAMSEEN   The desert wind, hot and dry.

KOHL   A cosmetic of the Orient, used on the eyelids and lashes to darken them.

LAPIS LAZULI   A semiprecious stone, azure blue in color.

LARES   Guardian spirits of the house, to protect the home from outside harm. See *penates*. The *lares* and *penates* were the center of worship in the house.

LEGATUS   Second in command, assisting the general.

LIBRA   A weight, about the same as our pound today. The abbreviation *lb.* comes from the word libra.

MIKVEH   A pool for purification. Used by men after defilement and by people when they convert to the Jewish religion. Used by women monthly. Used by all before the Sabbath and holy days.

MOHEL   The Jewish people follow the agreement made between Abraham and God that all male children should be circumcised. The mohel performs the ceremony.

PANTHEON   A temple for all the gods.

PARAPET   A wall in front of a walk or platform to protect those inside the fort during siege.

PAX ROMANA   Roman peace. No country dared to attack Rome or her allies. Thus there was peace for those who sided with Rome.

PENATES   Gods of the Roman household believed to be responsible for the safety within the house. See *lares.*

PHARISEES   A religious-political party which maintained that the Oral Law was quite as important as the Written Law (Torah). They were the majority party during the first century B.C.E. They asked for scrupulous belief in both Oral and Written Law.

PHYLACTERIES   A religious Jew today as in former days follows the commandment of praying to God every morning. To keep himself constantly reminded of the oneness of God, the worshiper fixes the words "Hear O Israel, the Lord our God, the Lord is One" on his forehead and on the arm nearest the heart. These small boxlike containers contain the *Shema* prayer.

PRINCEPS · Leader, chief; head of the Roman Senate.

SADDUCEES The religious-political party that opposed the Pharisees; composed mostly of priests, merchants, and aristocracy. They refused to accept the Oral Law. They did not believe in an afterlife, in angels or devils, or that man's life and future were decided by God.

SAPPERS Soldiers responsible for building forts and destroying enemy walls.

SHARDS Pieces of broken earthenware jar.

SHOFAR The horn of an animal used for calling the Jewish people together for religious purposes or other gatherings.

SICA A short, sharp dagger.

SICARIUS (pl. SICARII) A man who carried a *sica* and rebelled against Rome.

SPQR *Senatus populusque romanus* (The Senate and People of Rome), the initials on the banners of the Roman army.

STYLUS A pointed instrument for writing on wax.

TALENT Money of Greek and Roman times, probably worth $1,250.

TALIT   Jewish prayer shawl.

TESTUDO   A Roman military strategy used in attacking a fortified place. The legionaries locked their shields above their head like a large tortoise *(testudo)* shell.

TOGA   A loose outer garment worn in public by men of ancient Rome in time of peace.

WADI   Arabic for a valley through which a stream can flow.

ZEALOT   Jewish patriots that fought the Romans.